First of December

First of December

Karen Jennings

www.hhousebooks.com

Copyright © 2025 by Karen Jennings

Karen Jennings asserts her moral right to be identified as the author of this book. All rights reserved. This book or any portion thereof may not be reproduced or used in any manner whatsoever without the express written permission of the publisher except for the use of brief quotations in a book review.

This book is a work of fiction. Names, characters, places and incidents are either a product of the author's imagination or are used fictitiously. Any resemblance to actual people living or dead, events or locales is entirely coincidental.

Softcover ISBN: 978-1-0683164-1-8

Cover design by Ken Dawson

Typeset by Rachel Zadok

Published in the UK

Holland House Books
Holland House
47 Greenham Road
Newbury, Berkshire RG14 7HY
United Kingdom

www.hhousebooks.com

Historical Note

Slaves had been imported to the Cape by the Dutch East India Company since the seventeenth century. Most came from India and the East Indies, with only about a quarter coming from East Africa, Mozambique, and Madagascar. The local indigenous tribes of the Cape, now generally known as the Khoesan but then referred to as Hottentots, were never enslaved, however many were compelled to accept indentured servitude because of lost grazing land, depletion of herds, and tribes being wiped out by disease. The British took possession of the Cape in 1806, and in 1807 the Slave Trade Act prohibited the slave trade throughout the British Empire, though it did not prevent the practice of slavery. It wasn't until 1 August 1834 that slavery was abolished entirely in the Empire, taking effect in most colonies on 1 December of that year. In order to help ease the process of change, ostensibly for slaves and owners alike, a system was introduced whereby slaves were to be trained for freedom; they were known as apprentices and had to continue to serve their masters for a further four years. Some masters paid wages, others did not. Finally, on 1 December 1838, full emancipation of the slaves in the Cape Colony occurred. While slave owners were paid compensation by the British government, no such compensation or provision was given to the slaves themselves.

Sunday
25th November 1838

She left before they were all asleep. There was still a drunk, singing in the yard of the inn, too merry to find his way to bed and to sleep. She feared guards would come, and had already seen a window open, heard someone shout at the drunk that it was late, that he had better shut up or find himself in the naval lockup. She had not made it far from the doorway, taking only a step or two towards the water butt, crouching down behind it. The night was lighter than she had hoped it would be, stars bright, moon full and yellow. The wind howled around the yard, set shutters clapping against the walls of the inn, pails tumbling, chickens clucking in their coop. Still the drunk crooned. She watched him grab the coop, laugh to himself, saying, "What's this now, what's this?", following the slats all around and coming back to where he had begun. He laughed again and allowed himself to sink down, leaning against the coop, his head back, eyes closed, continuing with his song. She waited a while, saw him begin to nod forward, the singing coming to a stop, then moved slowly past him, keeping to shadows, until she reached the barn.

The cow was warm and sleeping, grunting low sounds at her entrance, far too early for milking, but it nudged her hand, let her smooth a palm over its soft nose. She felt pain at having to leave it. The loss of this warm body, this steady routine, every morning standing with her, through all the days of the year, this comfort. She began to think that she should not leave. Who would milk the cow come morning? Who would feed the chickens? But then the fear she had known all these months was with her again and she was grabbing in the straw for a bundle she had hidden earlier. An old cloak, torn, that had been left behind by a guest, hard crusts from a couple of stale loaves, three apples and six runner beans, two tomatoes, taken from the garden. She picked up the bundle, felt the lightness of it. It was nothing, so little, yet none of it was hers, all of it stolen, and she felt sick at the thought of it, wanted to drop it to the ground, thinking again of the comfort of milking.

She slipped back outside, careful to be quiet. The drunk was no longer asleep, had seen her move, and said, "Who's there, who's that?" She expected the window to open again, for someone to stick their head out, see her there in the moonlight with the things she had taken. But there was no sign that anybody had heard the drunk, and he seemed to be asleep again or near to it. She ran now, down the dirty, wagon-rutted path that led from the inn to the main road, and then along the edge of the main road to the far end of the town, away from the toll gate and the naval houses of Simonstown, out towards the graveyard. In her fear, she could not find the entrance, but the wall was low, and she climbed over the stones quickly, lying down when she got to the other side. The day had been hot and the ground was warm, despite the wind and the late hour. She lay there, felt the warmth on her arms and forehead, waiting for her breath to still.

After a while came the slow tramp of the patrol approaching along the road. She remained as she was, gripping the earth with her fingernails, holding her breath, wishing they would pass quickly. One of them said, "That's what they're saying." Then, "Wait a moment." Footsteps neared and halted on the other side of the wall, the sound of urine hitting stones, the smell of it strong enough to reach her.

"Do you think it will be as bad as all that?" the other one asked, beginning to walk again.

"Bound to be, wouldn't you say? Bound to be drinking and all sorts of goings on. They don't know how to behave, that's the problem. They've never been free, that's what he was saying. They don't know how to be free, and this thing, this change, it's going to be a violent business, I'm telling you."

She waited until she could no longer hear them, then turned on her side, seeing the bright sky, the starlit graves all around. It seemed a frightening place, with the threat of the dead rising up towards her. At the inn it was often spoken of. What travellers had seen on long, lonely roads, and encounters they had had in the dark of night with souls that were restless or angry, or simply lost. Whenever there was a death in town, the other slave women would whisper about it in the marketplace, warning everyone to lock windows and doors, and for weeks at a time took care not to call one another by name so that the ghost would not hear it, would not be able to identify them, rising from its grave and coming down into the town at night, trying to get in wherever it could, searching for a body to take possession of and drive into madness.

There had been a death a few days before. A young sailor newly arrived at Simonstown. That was all she had heard about it, all she knew, apart from the fact that he was dead and was to be buried. Running up to the main road at mid-morning, her hands wet and raw from scrubbing the floors, watching the funeral procession pass, the mourners, the coffin, and she wished the man alive again, or long since dead, fearing the timing of it, that in dying when he did, he would be waiting for her in the next few days, that he would come for her and that this would be her punishment for leaving, to be made sick with madness, to be taken over and forced out of herself.

She scanned the graves from where she lay in the dirt, looking for movement, and then started when she found it. It was true, then, all of it had been true. Here was the young sailor, here he was and he was coming for her. Yet he had lost his human form, appeared to be hunched over, walking on all fours, and he was monstrous, a horrific lumbering thing, coming for her. She slowly reached into her bundle, took out the food she had stolen, hoping that these few things would be enough, though the women in the market had spoken of ghosts being ravenous, demanding full meals, such as the living would eat. She pushed the bread and vegetables forward, her hands cold now, shaking as she drew them to her chest, closed her eyes, listening to the creature begin to make its way down through the graves towards her. From time to time it paused, made strange snuffling sounds, seemed to be digging, to be digging up the rest of the dead and bringing them to life. All of them coming for her, and nothing to give them but these few scraps. She opened her eyes, waiting to see the ghosts upon her, but there were none, every sound and movement gone. Sitting up, looking for it again, and there it was, coming out from behind a headstone, into the moonlight, and it was no shadowy being, no monstrous creature. It was only a porcupine, its quills shining silver in the starlight.

She rose at once, grabbing the food, returning it to her bundle, beginning to move through the graves, keeping low, the porcupine to her left. Twice she stopped, looked over towards it, making sure that it had not once more become monstrous, that it was not the dead sailor following her. It seemed a long time since she had left the inn and she worried that she would spend the whole night this way, in doubt and fear, making no progress. At last, she reached the far wall and climbed over it, the stones grating against one another, rough against her feet.

The incline had been gentle through the cemetery, but it was all steep from here, going straight up into the wilderness of the mountain. She had never been on this slope, never, that she could remember, been this far from the inn, had only ever seen the mountains spreading out behind the town and on into the distance. It was September who had known the mountain, he who had been sent out to collect firewood from the crooked shrubs and low trees. She had envied him that task. He came back always humming, smelling of fresh plants, of different soil, that smell still on him when they lay together at night, and she had drawn him close to her, taking deep breaths of that other life.

Here it was now, for her. The rocks, the coarse scrub, scratching her legs, her arms, even a few times making her pause, want to cry out a moment, thinking herself bitten or wounded. But this was September right here, this the earth and these the stones he had known, and she wondered if that was what he had done with his freedom, gone into the mountains and stayed there. Two years since she had last seen him. He had been beaten for staying out all night. There had been a storm and he had lost his way in the fog while looking for firewood, having to take shelter, and beaten for it when he came back. He did not wait to heal, went at once with his wounds, all the way along the wagon road, to Cape Town, to lay a complaint with the Special Justice because beatings weren't allowed any longer, not now that they were apprentices and not slaves. The master had let him go free rather than have the trouble of a case, saying he had already had his compensation money, so let him be done with this nonsense once and for all. The last time she had seen September, his face bruised, his back bleeding, trying to tend to him with a wet rag, trying to take the shirt off him, he had pushed her away, said only that he was going, and she watched him walk slowly up the dirt track, thinking at any moment that he would stop and she would run to him and help him to the barn, laying him down in the straw.

Wondering again whether she shouldn't go back, thinking of being caught, of being beaten. Her terrible fear, sitting inside her, this terrible fear of what she had done. She stopped, turned to face the village, listened for sounds, any, that might show that her absence had been noticed, that she was being pursued. But there was only the wash of the shore. Even that frightened her. She could smell the sea on the wind, smell the salt and sand, and she began to cry. She had been nowhere else, had heard at the inn what visitors said about the world, of other places, places where there was no sea, where there was none of this, and what was that world to her?

What could it be to her? Some days you could see across the bay, see the wagon road winding along the coast, and she had learnt from servants and slaves who had come with their masters to the inn the names of Elsie's Peak, of Muizenberg, but nothing beyond, not Cape Town which was out of sight, a foreign country for all she knew of it. Each morning pushing open the kitchen window, looking out to see if the view had changed, if it had brought places nearer or further, feeling the salt breeze on her face as she willed away the stuffiness of yesterday's onions. That view, that unaltering view. She would go back, to the kitchen table, the knife, the basins and plates. Go back, mend her dress where it had torn, open the window, scrub the table, milk the cow, feed the chickens.

There was the hush of the shore below, the wide-open night, and before her the silent darkness of the mountain, the sky bright and star-filled all around.

FIRST OF DECEMBER

Of the wreck nothing remained. There were only the waves, frothing under the southeaster that had blown for days on end. Clouds rushed across the sky, the sun coming and going, coming and going. By the time Caroline and James reached the Cape Town shore, it had gone once more, and everything dimmed a little, made dimmer still by the sand, lifted and flung across the beach by the wind. Already it was in her mouth, and she gathered saliva to swallow it down while he unfastened the veil on her bonnet and lowered it over her face. She could feel his breath on her cheek, the sting of sand at the gap between her gloves and blouse, though he had turned her away from the worst of it. The veil fell unevenly over one side of her brow and she raised a hand to adjust it. "Did I not do it properly?" he asked, and she brought her hand down again, said, "No, you did." In the distance the clanging of church bells began, then paused, began again, and faded.

Before them, the shore carried the burden of the town's waste. Stalks and peels, burnt scrapings from pots, bones gnawed bare, a mulch of fallen leaves, the swollen carcasses of dogs and cats, buckets of nightsoil, all making their slow way down the canals of the Heerengracht, before tumbling out onto the sand to mix with leavings from the nearby shambles and fish market. The beach was stained with it, a smear that lay shivering and brown wherever the waves spread it.

Packs of dogs dug through the rot, as did rats, dark and wet and bloated. Chickens wandered down from nearby fishermen's cottages, pecking fussily at what could be found. People had come too; the destitute, the hopeful, slave apprentices, freed men and women, orphans and foreigners; though little remained of the wreck now, the ship already gone for a day and a night. Yet there were still splinters of wood drifting in the dirty foam, here and there an item of clothing, a hat, or boot, or something else sodden and lost. Most of those who had come to the shore walked with sticks of one sort or another, poking the stained shore, the piles of waste. Others removed their shoes, wading out into the water to lift out bits of floating rope and wood, or bent over to thrust their hands into the sand and filter through it. Caroline could hear their cries, saw their looks of surprise when a wave caught them, splashing into their lowered faces. But one man, shirtless, the marks of his branding clear on his chest, remained upright. He moved slowly, frowning, looking out ahead of him where the coast turned away from the town. Then his frown deepened and he stood still, waving to a woman standing nearby. She came closer and he leaned on her shoulder, lifted one of his legs out of the water, toes clenched. The woman cupped her hands beneath his foot, and he dropped what he had found into them. It was too small for Caroline to see at this distance, but it seemed to be something of value by the way they huddled close to one another, their fingers smoothing the thing between them.

"For God's sake."

She looked up at the sound of James's voice, saw that he too had noticed the pair.

"For God's sake," he said again. Then, "Where is Stone? This should not be allowed. It is thievery, no less than thievery."

He took a step towards the water, but remembered her and

said, "I'm sorry, I must see to this," as though that had not been his intention all along. Why else had he brought them to this stinking place, leaving the Sunday service with greater haste than usual, and marching down the Heerengracht despite the southeaster blowing hard against them. She had not been able to push through it, could not keep up with his striding. From time to time he was compelled to pause, offer her his arm, his irritation clear in the way he did not look at her when he asked "Better now?" before striding on. She had begun to perspire, had felt it on her brow and lips, soaking through her chemise and marking her dress under the arms. It formed behind her knees too, made her feel both hot and cool, and she thought she might at any moment begin to shiver, or perhaps even faint, and grew afraid that she might be unwell again. Yet when James stopped to greet the gentlemen and ladies of their acquaintance, she responded to inquiries about her health with "Recovering quite well, thank you." James adding, as though he were ashamed of her slow pace, "A gentle stroll, by order of Dr Greene, but she's up and about now and as well as ever." Then he squeezed her elbow, or nudged her softly with his own, and she would say, "Oh, yes, I do so look forward to seeing you at our party on Friday."

On the beach James had begun to move her in the direction of the prison. An awning had been raised opposite, with sand raked clear beneath it. From one side of the wooden frame hung a flag of the London Missionary Society, jerking wildly before tearing free at a corner. A silver-haired preacher mounted an upturned crate, supported at each arm by a younger man, waiting as he coughed. Behind him waves thrust at the shore, throwing up sprays of white where they beat upon the rocks. The preacher continued to cough, turning to say something to one of the two men as he did. The man then called out to the sailors and apprentices, drunks and prostitutes who had gathered beneath the awning's shade. Overhead the canvas shook noisily, the frame creaking and shaking, while the wind continued to roar, flinging sand and debris at them. Still, there were those who had heard the command and took out their hymnals, though few possessed them and fewer still could read. The rest whispered amongst themselves, passing back the number and name of the hymn they were to sing. It began slowly, without accompaniment, and was taken up drearily, seeming to be only half known, and sung unevenly, the wind carrying snatches from one end of the congregation to the other, so that they felt ever out of rhythm, and unable to catch up.

James had his hand still on the small of her back, pushing her towards the congregants. She wished he would stop, let her lean against him and rest her head. She could no longer lift her feet, felt them dragging through the wretched sand. But he pushed on, making his way to where a few men and women were seated on stools.

"How much to sit down?" he said.

An old man, his dark face made darker by years of sun, said, "Well, sir, I'm not so far gone that I can't offer a lady a seat when she's in need."

He stood up, slow and stiff. She saw the bandages around his knees, the difficulty with which he moved, and she wanted to tell him that she was not in need, that she could easily stand, and he must, please, sit back down. But she felt still the threat of illness, felt the tremor of fever within her, and watched him bend forward, wipe the stool with his neckerchief, then offer her the seat with an open hand, his fingers calloused and broad and scarred.

She nodded at him, smiling a little, dizzy with the pressure of James's hand on her shoulder, pushing her down, the seat low so that she felt she was falling, falling and certain to faint. There was not enough air, she could not fill her lungs. She gripped the folds of her skirt, looking at them in fright. They seemed awash with colour and movement. She could not focus on the pattern, rows of small flowers, she knew them, could remember them, but could not see them. They would not remain still. Above her James was speaking, "… of pickpockets, understand?" Then he was striding out into the wind, and she was left with her hands clutching at those seething patterns. Around her the final words of the hymn echoed as the congregants slowly, individually, reached the end. She closed her eyes, felt the perspiration cool and settle. Something was being said, murmurs of assent came, and she found herself nodding too, nodding her way out of her panic and into calm.

The nodding spread to the rest of her, set her rocking as though upon water. She knew herself to be asleep because she had been cast adrift amongst a rush of waves, the sky a disturbance of stars overhead, and knew all of this to be impossible, impossible, not while she was still aware of the awning and the congregants around her. Yet she dreamt, seeing the wreck of the Dunlop tilting heavily bow-ward where it had run aground. Men dropped into the water in a bid to swim ashore, while women and children wailed at the stern. Far away, men in breeches and shirtsleeves shoved rowboats into the surf, struggling against the froth of waves, making little progress and almost certain to be taken under. Despite knowing herself to be dreaming, she too was being drowned, and it was certain that she would not be reached in time by the rescuers, her dress heavy, her arms weak. Stars became a shimmer, a blur, a nothing, as she gave in to the violence of the waves.

But then there was a hand on her arm, and she was awake, blinkingly awake, looking with confusion at a book being held out to her, at pages of text that she could not place.

"Beg pardon, ma'am, would you like to share?"

It was the woman who had been seated beside her, standing now, hymnal in hand. Around them the first line was already being sung: "Ah wither should I go, burdened and sick and faint?" She rose without thinking, took the corner of the hymnal with the tips of her fingers and looked down at it, still adjusting to wakefulness. She could not seem to form words, managing only to move her lips, while beside her the woman sang full heartedly. Caroline watched her turn the page, the lyrics sung loudly in her ear: "Some cursed thing unknown..."

She felt once more the waves upon her, the agitation of her drowning, and she wanted to shake herself free of it, to feel something else, something immense and stirring, anything, anything. Only let it be something beyond this dirty town and its ugly church and sad fashions, something warm and different. She let go of the hymnal, sat back down, grasped her hands in her lap.

But it was too much, she could take it no more, and she rose. She nodded at the woman, murmured her thanks with cast-down eyes to the man who had given up his stool for her, then pushed forward into the congregation. She could smell them, the sweat and alcohol on some, soap and pomade on others. They seemed to matter, these smells, to speak of something important, of life, of living, and she felt again a call to something, some great thing that needed to happen. She leaned forward with her yearning, pressing closer to the man in front of her, so that she fancied she could feel the warmth of his body on her bodice, smell his private scent behind the pomade and starch.

Ahead of them the preacher had once more mounted the crate. He spoke hoarsely, stopping to cough, then spoke again. "And they said to one another, We are verily guilty concerning our brother, in that we saw the anguish of his soul, when he besought us, and we would not hear; therefore is this distress upon us."

Though she was close enough to hear him, she did not listen. Instead, she paid attention to the breaths and murmurs of those around her. She could hear the softly whistling nose of the man in front of her, see the white flakes in his hair, on his shoulders. Her head felt heavy and weak. She wanted to lean forward, rest her forehead between those shoulders, feel the coarse fibres of his Sunday jacket pressing into her skin, smell the life of him.

"Conscience smote them for having sold their brother into slavery," the preacher said. "Sold and transported, without having committed any crime or done any evil. Transported, I say, to a foreign land to wear out his life in bitter bondage. That anguished soul called upon our heads to plead his cause, and the cause of myriad others. It is a relief to my heart and befitting of my office as servant of Him who came to preach liberty that the day is almost arrived, this day for which so many of us have fought and prayed. God's mercy be upon us."

The man in front of her nodded. "God's mercy," he said, and his voice was not what she had expected. Higher perhaps, and gentler. It should have been rough, coarse as his jacket. She looked at the woman beside him, short, her face red and clean. Between them stood a girl. All three nodded at the preacher's words, wore the same coarse clothing. Caroline was aware of her own fine dress. The skirt, which before had been such a blur of motion, now stood solidly around her. So wide was it that it touched each of them, the whole family. It seemed to be an extension of herself, as though she had held her arms out to them, embraced them all. She began to nod along with them, to add her murmur of assent to theirs, ready to go home with them, share their meals, their space, their thoughts and exertions.

"Come the first of December the chains will be broken for good," the preacher said. "Guilty we have been, but the Lord our God has seen fit that we should not continue to live in our guilt. We come to liberty, I say, we come to freedom!"

"Yes," she murmured along with the family, but then

the wind picked up suddenly and the congregants were turning away from it and the rushing sand. She had moved too far, was no longer touching the family. They seemed now a great distance from her, had become strangers. She felt once more the waves around her, the wild, churning threat of death. The family was gone and she was alone, struck blind by the sun on the water and that fierce call of the waves, drowning again, drowning.

James had gone down to the shore the night of the wreck, dressing quickly in the dark at the sound of the alarm, before running out into the Heerengracht, where already people were moving in disarray. He had walked briskly, tapping with his cane at the legs of those who had stopped to wait for one another, saying, "Mind there, if you please, move along", taking a moment to call up to the widow Cloete as she put her nightcapped head from her second-storey window, "Shipwreck, there's been a wreck!", his throat catching at the last word in his excitement. Moving on, swallowing hard before whispering the words again, "There's been a wreck," saying them evenly now, as he ought to have done before.

Yet the energy was still there when he reached the narrow shore. Men and women dashed from nearby cottages, calling for blankets, for hot water, for soup to be made, for people to get out the way, get out the way there, as rowboat after rowboat was picked up by bands of men and pushed or carried out into the waves. Dogs, chained in backyards, had set to howling, while a few, broken free, ran about, barking and jumping in their excitement.

The ship sat dark and low in the wind-churned water. Brands continued to be lit but went out almost at once. Where he stood, James could hear the cries of those on board, all the desperate voices made the same by the wind, one long wail snapped into unequal parts, and with each part's abrupt end it was as though the same life were being taken again and again.

For what remained of the night, he stayed on the shore, pacing. He had sent for Stone, had given commands that men and boats be ready to go in afterwards and save what they could of the cargo. His eyes burned with watching, his feet burning too, and he could no longer carry on his restless striding. As dawn turned to day, he allowed himself at last to sit on one of the steps in front of the Port Office, putting his head down, holding it in his hands, but unable to close his eyes, so violent remained the urgency within him. He continued awake, staring without seeing at the filthy sand beneath his legs. Then someone was beside him, was addressing him softly. "Master can go home now." Looking up and not knowing her, a washerwoman or maidservant or someone of that sort. "What?" he said.

"Master can go home, it's over. Everyone saved, not a soul lost, everyone safe on dry land."

Again, he looked at her, could not understand what she had said, but "Not a soul lost?" he repeated.

"That's right, master, not a one, praise the Lord. Master can go home."

Dropping his head into his hands again, he closed his burning eyes. He was tired. No lives had been lost, and he was tired. Looking up slowly, out across the sea that was broadening under the morning light. Already the ship was starting to break up, to scatter and vanish. There was nothing to stay for.

He walked home heavily, waving off greetings in the street with a tired hand, shaking his head when asked questions. He would not talk now. "I must go home first," he said. "I must rest." But he did not rest, going straight to the breakfast room where Caroline was seated.

"Is there coffee? Where's the coffee?" glancing around the room, seeing nothing of it, as though the place had been overtaken by shadow. Feeling for a chair, holding it with both hands, letting them slide down the wooden back and onto the upholstered seat. He was not sure of what to do, knew Caroline was watching him, knew her to be watching these movements of his, waiting for him to do something ordinary, but he did not know what it was or how, until she said quietly, "Will you sit?" and it was enough only to have those words between them for him to remember how to do it.

She leaned across the table, serving him when the girl didn't come quickly enough. He could hear the coffee being poured, the cup and saucer being placed near his hand, the sugar being offered to him, being held out to him for a long time it seemed, and him staring at it, then taking it from her at last with both hands and putting it down beside the saucer. She asked where he had been and it was much simpler to tell her than to lift the cup to his lips, simpler to say there had been a wreck and that he had been at the shore. But suddenly he was furious, suddenly he detested her, knowing exactly what she would ask next, knowing but still angered by it, and waiting for her to form the words, to ask it, her little question. No, he said very quietly in reply. No one had died. But she had to make it worse, had to say in her breathless way, "Oh, thank goodness", as though she had known any of the passengers and crew, as though she had had family and friends amongst them, as though she cared at all. He could stomach nothing after that, leaving her to eat alone.

Several times throughout Saturday he had returned to the shore, checking on his men and the salvage operation, each time his eyes going first to the shallows, because he could not rid himself of the thought that perhaps there had been some mistake, someone unaccounted for, and he expected to see that person floating in the surf, waiting to be found. But there were no corpses, and their absence seemed a betrayal. The wreck had been a promise, something had been promised him, though he did not know what, only that it had been pinned to the urgency inside him, that the two had been together, and nothing had come of it.

Again last night he had not slept, rising this morning with an aching head, the pain so great that all through the church service he had had to bite down. Now, on the shore once more, having left Caroline under the awning of the Missionary Society, the brightness of sunlight reflecting sharply off the water making the pain even greater, he fought to ignore it, it was not part of him, not this weakness, and he strode on, though everything he looked upon was unrecognisable. He did not know this filth and chaos, this shore which appeared to have been stretched out overnight, reaching towards places he could not remember. Still, he followed the thin curve of sand, coming to the low wall of the fish market, knowing it by the stench, by the litter of fish heads and scales, and the coarse calls of those few who were still left selling their Sunday wares. Beside the wall, on the sand, were boats. Slave apprentices sat in them, mending and caulking, or stood about, talking amongst themselves. They did not move when James neared, remained silent, some of them glaring, others with their arms folded across their chests. He had not brought his cane with him today, would have struck them with it, was ready to, raising his arm even, but "Move!" was all he could do, and then again "Move!", the flow catching him, filling his shoes as he waited for them to step aside in their sullenness.

Walking away from them stiffly, feeling still the weight of his cane in his hand, clenching his fingers, then seeing Stone standing nearby, writing with a pencil in a notebook, three small crates stacked beside him. James did not greet him as he approached, felt lightheaded, could not quite catch his breath, could feel still the slaves' hard eyes on him. He leaned against the top crate, motioned at Stone to be quiet, to give him a minute, then brought that same hand up to his eyebrows, pressing down on them as he turned towards the ground, away from the light and the wind. For a time it was only the pain that he saw, then slowly, as he continued with his pressing, he began to lift out of it, managed to master himself.

But there were his shoes, his best shoes, put on in error that morning, now wet and filthy in the sand. He ought to have changed them, ought to have gone home after the service, giving Caroline a moment to sit down and rest, perhaps even to lie down for a quarter of an hour. She would have needed that, he knew, needed it now, in fact, and he looked over towards the awning as though to confirm how tired she was, but it was too far to see anything other than the tattered flag.

He took a handkerchief from his pocket, bent down and began to clean his ruined shoes. There was no way of replacing them in time for the party. He had bought them in London some months before, under the recommendation of Lord Inglesby, who had told him there was no finer shoe and bootmaker to be had than Moore's. It was Lord Inglesby's approval that he had particularly sought on that visit, hoping that this old friend of the family would forget James's early misfortunes, as well as the rift they had caused between himself and his father and brothers, that he would introduce him to possible investors for the bank James planned to open in the new year, one of the first private banks in the colony.

"What do you think will happen to the emancipated?" James had said to him. "Do you imagine they will disappear? There will be 6 000 in Cape Town alone, easily another 30 000 in other districts, and do you think they'll want to remain in the countryside when there is the possibility of a better life waiting for them in town? Of course not! Within no time at all, they will have arrived in their numbers, providing a new workforce, a workforce that is earning in cash and that is going to have money for spending in a way that we have never seen before. There's opportunity there, opportunity for the taking, and already the Cape is changing, the very town is changing shape with new buildings and enterprises, thanks to the compensation funds that came in. It is becoming a city, and we can be part of making that happen, we can shape it and control it. Believe me, never has the time been better for investing in the future of the Cape."

He turned now to Stone. "Well, how much?"

Stone wrote something in his notebook. "Hard to know until I've seen the manifest. I'll get it from the captain today or tomorrow."

"But more or less?"

He shrugged, put the pencil behind his ear. "You've seen

the wind, can't salvage much when it's like this. We got what we could yesterday before it broke up."

"And these?" James tapped at the three small crates with the tip of his shoe.

"Found this morning. One here in the shallows, two in rockpools."

"Anything of value?"

Stone pointed at the top crate. "Lacquered boxes. Haven't looked in the others yet."

The top crate had been damaged in the wreck and bore now a large crack in its lid. James lowered his head to it. There was the smell of swollen wood, of sand, and something else, perhaps of a breath held in, of something cold and alive. Only as he turned his head did the contents begin to reveal their mother-of-pearl peacocks and willows and castles. He thought of previous salvage auctions, trying to remember what a lot such as this might have gone for, but it was difficult to say without first assessing the damage. If they had become waterlogged, if they were warped and cracked and came apart, he would sell them in one lot. Cheap. But if there was little distortion, perhaps two lots, or even three, get a bit more for them. He wondered what other goods had been recovered, and in what state they might be. "Make sure you have been through the manifest properly," he said to Stone. "I want to be certain of what we have and what has been lost."

It was that which rankled most, everything that was missing. All those crates and sacks and piles of stock, going down with the ship, landing somewhere along the seabed, out of reach, where the contents would eventually disintegrate,

or become the homes of various sea creatures, barnacle-
-ridden, pest-laden, wasted. Or worse, a crate might break
open, as this one had, and the currents work at the contents,
lure them outside, tumble them in the grit of sand and shells
and bones, the faces of clocks rubbed smooth, silverware
moulded into odd shapes and freed from their hallmarks.
Washing up one day upon a shore, at some unknown distance,
where he would be powerless to prevent those dull knives
and churned spoons from being picked up and taken home,
made into treasures, heirlooms. Or, the very worst, picked
up and sold, with profit being made where no risk had been
taken.

Already they were here, the mudlarks and scavengers,
all around him, up and down the beach. Though he had
his back to them, he could feel their searching eyes, their
desperate hands, filtering through the debris, grasping at the
waves, taking everything, everything before them. He expected to turn, have their hideous breaths in his face, their violent
need all around him as they tore at his clothes, his hair,
his flesh, pushing through him to the crates and the lacquered
boxes.

"Clear this lot off," he said.

Stone had resumed writing in his notebook, but he looked up now. "Ah, leave them be. There's nothing of value
left now."

"No? What is this then?" He pointed at the crates. "Where
did these come from?"

Stone said nothing.

"I want every rockpool searched; I want every inch

of shoreline checked. Send men that way, round past the hospital."

"We've already checked there."

"And beyond? Have you been to Green Point? And what about in the other direction? I want this entire coastline scoured."

"Sir, that is—"

"And I want the beaches cleared of these scavengers. God knows what they have already managed to make off with."

Stone shook his head and walked across the sand to where three men were hunched over, smoking pipes in the shelter of the fish market wall. He spoke to them, pointing to each in turn. The first stood up as soon as Stone's finger landed on him, going in the direction of the hospital. The other two had rifles slung over their shoulders and they rose more slowly, seemed reluctant to do what had been asked of them. One of them was a coloured man and he held the rifle in front of him, shaking it like a stick, saying quietly, "Move along, move along. Come on, off with you." The other, redheaded, no more than a boy, stood still a moment, loading the rifle, then walked out to the middle of the beach and fired into the air. Around him, people began to scream, moving away as he recharged and fired once more. He motioned to his partner to come along, and together now, some ten yards apart, they stalked the shore. The coloured man continued to wave his rifle before him, sometimes holding it in the air with the threat of firing, though he never did, only telling everyone to move along, as quietly as before.

James had left the crates, walked now at a distance behind the rifled men, watching as the scavengers began to scatter. Amongst them he saw the pair he had noticed before with Caroline, the branded man, the woman at his side, saw them hastening with difficulty out of the shallows, alarmed by the shots, clutching hold of one another. They saw the redheaded boy ahead of them, tried to get behind him. He saw them too, turned and thrust the rifle at them, his mouth wide as he shouted for them to go on, get along, move it, move it. But the woman was weighed down by her drenched skirts and could not move, was stumbling, stumbling, the man pulling at her arm, holding her up, moving her forwards. Then she was down, could not rise, and James saw the man turn, saw his face now, the grim expression and strain as he tried to pull her to her feet. She had begun digging in the dirty sand with her free arm, snatched the other from him and dug with that too. He bent down, spoke, but the woman did not seem to listen, only shouted something at him, and his grim expression changed to one of panic. He threw himself down beside her, put his hands into the filth that lay there, both of them scrabbling in it. But then the boy was upon them once more, had come back to them, shouting, pointing his rifle at the sky, telling them to move on, move on. The man stood, held outstretched empty hands to the boy, then bent down again, pleading with the woman. She continued digging in the sand. The boy avoided the woman, but he kicked the man in his back, on his thigh, shouted until he had risen. The man took hold of the woman's arm, pulling at it, and it seemed she would not rise, she would stay looking in the sand, but then there was rifle fire and she was up and screaming, even with the wind James could hear the screaming, and the woman was up, stumbling forward, the man dragging her by the arm.

James walked towards the spot where they had fallen. There were patches of damp from where the woman had sat, her skirts leaching into the sand. He began to trace the damp with the toe of his shoe, then moved beyond it, going through the loose sand where she had been digging, breaking up clumps with his foot. There was nothing, nothing at all, he could find nothing. And then there it was, a clot of sand that would not give way under pressure. He bent over to pick it up. Just then a strong gust knocked him forward and he was on his hands and knees in the dirt as she had been. The clot was gone, he could not see it. But no, there it was again, there beside his palm, and he picked it up, felt the lightness of it, no weight to it at all, rubbing it between his hands, chafing the sand off until he could see what it was.

A button, a brass one. No more than that. Worthless. Still, he blew the last of the sand from it, placed it in an inside pocket, then stood and wiped down his knees and the sleeves of his jacket, angry that he might have been seen. Looking over the cleared beach, towards the clamour now in the streets beyond, but there were no eyes on him, only on the men and their rifles, at the scavengers moving up, away from the shore.

All the while the wind was blowing strong, and he had to turn from the sand that was stinging against his cheek. Seeing again the Missionary Society awning as he turned, having forgotten it, forgotten Caroline sitting beneath it. He could not see her, she was not where he had left her, and he took a step forward, ready to call to the men with their rifles to go find her, she was missing, but then he saw her, standing pale and silent amongst the singing throng. He began to walk towards the awning, the words in his mind already, the tone, so that he could hear himself, grabbing her, leading her away, saying, "When I tell you to do something it is not for my sake. You know what is coming, there may well be riots and assaults and murders, and where will you be? For once, Caroline, just for once, listen to me and do as I say."

Seeing her clenched jaw, watching her all the way, anger building up within him, again and again that anger, and then she turned and was staring straight at him. He stood still. Stared back. Her mouth had opened a little, her eyes bright and wide, her expression always so sharp, so severe, now soft, all the hard lines and angles of her face softening as she looked at him, and his anger went away, seeing her love and admiration.

Yet it was not her alone. All eyes were on him, all of that throng, pointing and staring, and he put his hand suddenly to the pocket where the button lay, as though it were that at which they were looking, that and his humiliation in the sand. But it was not him they saw, not even Caroline had noticed him. They were looking beyond him, to the water. He turned, realised then what had caught their attention. A long streak of cormorants, hundreds and hundreds of them, darkening the sky and water. They flew low, landing on the waves, rising just as they touched it, so that the great dark shadow was in continuous motion, changing shape, a thing that could not remain still, and it kept going in that fashion, half on water, half in the air, all along the bay and round the bend, out of sight.

Monday
26th November 1838

She woke to a door slamming, windows rattling. The night was warm, and she had been sleeping restlessly as it was, aware of the southeaster shrieking, pushing through spaces between buildings and down streets and avenues. Around her there was darkness, the heavy curtains drawn tight. She stared into it with wide eyes until it began to take on shapes, to fill out with colours and landscapes; places from her life or others only imagined. There, where she knew her wardrobe to be, stood the silhouette of a lemon tree. There, approaching it, the boy-form of James, from a memory he had once shared of being lifted up by a woman who was not his mother and how he had been allowed to pick a ripe lemon. How he had refused to give it up, keeping it with him for weeks, in his pocket, or under his pillow at night. She placed her hand under her own pillow, expecting in that moment to find the same lemon there, surprised when there was none.

Kicking the sheet away from her, the room thick with heat, lighting the candle beside her bed, watching the banality of her bedroom emerge out of the lemon tree. Red shadows cast across her view, borrowing their colour from the curtains, the flame, the heavy air. All the while the windows and doors continued to clatter, to clatter, to beat at her, until her head ached with the rhythm, and she rose frantically, taking the candle with her. Fleeing into the passage, down the stairs, entering other rooms, leaving them again, everything glowing and shadowing in different tones, so that she moved from redness to redness, barefoot across floorboards and rugs and animal skins. Somewhere beyond the shrieking wind a pack of stray dogs had begun to howl. She wondered whether James was awake, hearing the same mournful sounds. Those cries binding them to one another at this hour, to this fierce and red night.

But red had been all her nights, red even her days. Seven years since they had arrived at the Cape, seven years of yearning for home, walking around with that feeling as strong as heartbreak, that nothing was right, and that nothing would be right again. Not on this promontory where words she had always known had been used to name flowers and creatures that she did not recognise, mingling with phrases and terms she could not understand, strange leftovers from the Dutch who had governed before. Them, or the natives, or any of the multitude of foreigners who seemed to have been spat out here at the bottom of the globe. The customs seemed makeshift, to have risen out of the unpaved streets, the hollers of passersby, or to have alighted, fractured, from visiting ships. It seemed impossible to her, all this, a world turned on its head, where winter rains flooded the town in July, and the New Year's sun parched the already suffering croquet lawn, burnt the edges of hydrangeas. A world in which she had no part. Every day her longing for home pulsed within her like desire.

Three times James had been back home, knowing how much she wished to join him, yet with each visit he had left her behind, explaining that he went for business, not leisure, that she would be a hindrance to him. He had seen an opportunity to branch out from his marine salvage company, to act as an agent, collecting slave compensation money from the government for the many owners in the colony who could not go themselves. "This is it," he had said. "This will change everything, you'll see." But what was there to see, what, other than her captivity? Knowing the reason why she could not accompany him, the real reason, the one he would never dare say, that once, in anger, she had shouted, had said she could not be expected to stay here, to live in this place, in this way, not after all his lies and promises. She wanted her money, she had said, all of it, wanted it now, and she would go back home, would be happy if she never set eyes on him again.

Living in Buitenkant Street then, in a small house in the unfashionable part of town, near his warehouse in Boom Street. He had bought Leah shortly after their arrival, and they had a freedman for a cook, as well as an orphan boy who came in most days to do odd jobs. There were few neighbours apart from the soldiers at the Great Barracks across the way. Nothing to do in the long weeks of James's absence, nothing but stand at the window, watching the soldiers on the parade ground, coming to know their manoeuvres as though she were one of them, anticipating the next step, shifting her shoulders and feet as they did. This shared rhythm followed them into the streets, reaching into their voices as they wandered past in small groups. Their accents varied, yet each reminded her of home, and those voices became her own, it was her out there whistling at the grey sky, going about in the world, understanding and belonging.

There were the prostitutes too, ones of mixed race

who loitered in the street outside the barracks; some of them pretty, many of them not, yet all of them dressed in bright colours, and cackling with similar rough lustiness. Sometimes they would fight amongst themselves, spit and scratch, pull hair, rip clothes. Sometimes they were drunk, and lay passed out in the street, where soldiers kicked them up, moved them on. Several times daily these same soldiers would stop and talk to the women, and a blouse might be opened or a skirt lifted so that they could see what was on offer, and pairings would occur. Rather than disgust her, these moments increased her sense of longing, not only for home, but for James, for affection, so that when he returned that first time, having made the money to buy the big house in the Heerengracht where they now lived and about which he had said, "Surely this is enough like home", she had hoped he might once more share a bed with her, or at least visit it at night. But no such visit occurred, and she wondered where he went some evenings, trying to imagine him with one of these bright-skirted women, leaning against the cold stone wall of a dirty alleyway, his breath quick with wanting.

And yet, "I did not forget you," he had said after that first trip home, three hired men bringing a tall, narrow crate into the parlour, James following behind saying, "In there, in there." One of the men had taken a crowbar to the wood, splitting the sides, and the men had leaned in, pulling out thickly packed straw, letting it drop to the floor.

"See what I've brought for you," he said, as the men lifted the harp onto the rug. He walked around it, pulled straw from the strings. "Second best available, and I have it on good authority that no less a person than Lady Burnham has one."

"But I do not play."

"I don't believe there is another as fine as this in the colony."

"You used to tease me about how unmusical I am. My fingers were made of stone, that is what you said."

"Caroline." He spoke slowly. "I went to a great deal of trouble to bring this across the ocean for you. You say you are bored. You say you have nothing to do. Here, right here, is something for you to do."

She had written to her sister, begged her to send the cold cream, soap, all the things she had asked James to bring and which he had been too busy to purchase. Then having to bear the humiliation of the letter that accompanied their arrival months later. "Are you then such savages in the colonies that you cannot wash?" and "How quaint your expressions have become, Carrie, I assure you we puzzle over them for hours and try to play at guessing what you might be saying. I shall require a dictionary before too long. It can hardly be a civilized place if these are the things you are compelled to say and do. Are we to expect, should you ever return, that you have been transformed into a native, with clothes of fur and garbled speech, communing with monkeys and elephants and other such animals?" And, finally, the postscript: "I shall not mention this to Mother, it will upset her greatly; pray, do not write to her on the matter."

No, to her mother she wrote of visits with the ladies of the Cape; the governor's wife, the brides of churchmen and officials, daughters of medalled officers; giving details of teacakes that she cribbed from her sister's letters, writing of fashions and other topics in a similar way, or else relying on outdated magazines and newspapers which took months to arrive by ship. She said nothing of the nearby grog shop, of drunks roaming the streets day and night, of how some mornings the smell they left in the alley near the house was unspeakable, of the heathens of all colours who thrived here in their godlessness, despite the endless arrival of missionaries from abroad. She did not explain that rich and poor lived side by side much of the time, that it was possible for a house with a fine façade to be neighboured by the tumbledown dwelling of a freedman as black as pitch, or a judge to be cursed with a Mohammedan tailor next door. Every street seemed to be overburdened by the coarse Dutch and their fat daughters, or people of small means who brought broken stools outside to sit upon, as partially clothed children ran about, unminded, ready to be knocked down by passersby, or snatched away by stray dogs. They sat, many of them haggard with disease and age, spitting and hacking as the women dressed one another's hair, all of them scratching and flea-bitten.

And into this he had brought her, continued to bring her, over and over again. "Here," he had said, only a few months before, leading her onto an expanse of swampy ground, thick with weeds and rubbish. "Our new house." At the back of the property stood a small cottage. Part of the thatched roof had fallen in, birds flying in and out of its two rooms. He pushed open the door, stepped aside to let her enter first. She shook her head, took out a handkerchief and held it to her nose. He bowed deeply, said, "After you, my lady," smiling as though it were a game, but it was no game, the place was rotten, vile. She would not enter, shook her head, took a step back, half-turning to look away, across the wasteland, back towards the street, to their house just around the corner on the Heerengracht.

"We have a house," she said.

"This one will be better."

Putting out his hand for her to take, and she knew he was angry by the way it trembled, the way he continued to smile. She stepped forward, clasped the handkerchief to her chest. She would not take his hand. She would enter the cottage, but she would not take his hand. The doorway was low and she ducked to enter, still looking back towards the street, the top of her bonnet brushing against the lintel, crumbs of wood falling on her shoulders. Inside, the walls were black with mould and soot, the thatch disintegrating, the floor sticky with decay.

"I have plans for it," he said, waving now with the hand he had been holding out to her before, showing her the extent of his vision. It was to be knocked down, he was going to build something large and impressive, to his own design, something that would rival the best they had in London and Bath. Throughout the town he would be known by this new house, by its grandeur and size.

Continuing now with her night's wandering through the house, wishing she could sleep, if only she might sleep, but that clattering, that endless clattering, the shrieking wind, the dreadful shrieking, and no way of resting, no way of coming to a moment of silence. Closing her eyes, the red of the night continuing behind her lids, and she was back in her room, back in that bed, back in her illness, feeling Leah nearby on the bedroom floor, wrapped in a blanket, her eyes opening at any sound from Caroline, rising, coming to her with water, a damp cloth. Leah who sent for Doctor Greene, because James had gone home, and there was no one but Leah to care for her. Leah who stood behind the doctor as he leaned over Caroline, holding her wrist, touching her forehead, mumbling into her face that she had typhus. But the words meant nothing to her. She had come from too far away, the struggle to reach this moment of consciousness too great. Too tired to speak, to hear, to try to make herself understood. Coming out of that long, dark tunnel, always into this same room, this bed, the red curtains, the oil painting of a forest glade, which was not hers, which had come with the house. Struggling into that which never changed, that emptiness, that frightful emptiness. Clawing her way out of the dark, where there was no floor, no ceiling, no walls, that rotten cottage, that petrifying mess, which grew, was ever growing, the sound of its growth all around her. That was where she lived in the dark of her sickness, that was where she struggled from, that taste of rubble and dust and decay, that brickwork collapsing and rising all around her.

Moving on into the parlour, wind still at the windows and doors, and she put the candlestick down upon the mantlepiece, looked around the room at waking shadows. There were decorative items brought back from the Eastern Frontier and the war being fought there. Such things were popular, were seen in every fine home, so James had bought a surplus of them – skins upon the floor and on the backs of couches and chairs, assegais mounted on walls, or leaning idly beside the fireplace, beadwork and strange items of clothing, no more than flaps of skin. Amongst these there hung tapestries she had made when she was younger, porcelain figurines and glass vases brought from home. Each of these she picked up, felt the weight of them in her hand, then set them down again. They were gritty to the touch, coated in dust from the building works around the corner, swept into the house by the ceaseless wind. She wiped her hands on her nightdress. There remained behind smeared fingerprints of ochre-coloured dirt, as though she had dipped her hands in blood.

FIRST OF DECEMBER

One night deep inside a dream, grasping after the nugget in the surging river, waking cold, alone, a cry still in his throat, then hearing her soft knock at the kitchen door, and wanting nothing more than to call to her, let her come in and hold him, but unable to bring himself to say a word. Perhaps there was something reassuring in that memory now, of frozen hands and feet, of struggling with that gold, because hadn't it been towards something? Wasn't this what he had done? Become a man people were proud to know, a man with a seven-bedroom cottage and a four-bedroom house, with another one coming, a bigger one, better, in which each room would have its own brass bed and fireplace. Rooms in which he would never be cold.

She had fallen in the night, struggling to see in the dark, in the howling wind that beat at her from all sides and made her eyes stream. Already she had tripped a few times, or caught herself stumbling in moments of half-sleep. She dreamed herself in other places, saw faces, heard talking. She was back at the inn, was making beds, pouring arak for drunk sailors, never for more than a few seconds at a time, always startling back into the mountain and the wind. She had been climbing up a crag, but in her dreaming she was carrying a pail of water across the yard. The pail was heavy, her arm straining at the weight. She reached out to push the kitchen door open, felt it give way at her touch, but it was not wood, was not the door. It was a loose outcropping of rock that came away as she put pressure on it. She could not catch hold of anything else, the weight of the pail holding back her other hand. She knew herself to be falling, still half-thinking herself in the yard and expecting to land in the soft dirt. But when she landed it was on rock, face down, one of her legs twisted beneath her. Struggling for breath, rolling herself onto her back, the sky above her unstable, stars blinking and fading, everything seeming to shift, to be moving, moving, and feeling herself to be moving too, to be still falling, to be losing her balance and falling, trying to push the door open and unable to enter.

Pain was slow to come, then leapt out across her body all at once. She sat up with difficulty, put both hands to the ankle that had been beneath her, felt already the heat and swelling, the roar that crawled up her leg, sat fluttering in her stomach, her chest. Not this, not this, here, alone in the dark. Her chin

Often he slept badly, waking confused, thinking himself back in the canvas tent in Mecklenburg County on the Carolina Piedmont, the day already hot, pricking at him, his body aching from the digging, the panning, from insufficient food, from heat and disappointment. Sleeping in his tattered clothes, the rest of his wardrobe and possessions long since pawned. Nothing left but the papers saying he had paid his share of 300,000 dollars for a charter for a mining company, all of it turning out to be false, the charter, the company, the partners. Only the gold was there, that at least was real, and he had no other option but that, to turn to prospecting and try to make something of himself. Rolling over in bed, still feeling the hard earth beneath him, his lips dry and cracked, raised flakes catching at one another. Reaching for his water canteen, finding instead of leather and tin a glass carafe, bringing it to his lips, drinking it down, spluttering, unable to swallow fast enough, then falling back into sleep within seconds, and he had risen from his blankets, had left the tent, was sifting his findings by the stream. This he knew, dreamt it repeatedly over the years, the stream, the pan, the gravel and dirt, his ribs pressing into his knees as he hunched over, searching, searching, and then there it was, a large nugget, big as a fist. Knowing it to be a dream, always the same, but telling himself that this time he would get it, this time – yet he would slip, or stumble, or be knocked over, something would happen and the gold was falling into the stream which had become a rushing torrent, impossible to wade into, to put his hands into and try to grab the gold that had already washed away. Waking angry, stiff and aching, the fury and rage of this loss again. Walking lock-kneed across the bedroom, a hand on his lower back, trying to will himself into the present, into a body without pain. He had left the chamber pot on the washstand during the night, and he picked it up now, urinating carefully into what was already there. It filled, and he leaned down with difficulty, watching as the movement made the contents tilt, spill a little onto the floor.

He opened the curtains, put a palm to the window, feeling the cool of the early morning, looking out, wanting to make sure of where he was. The glass fogged around the tips of his fingers, leaving a brief outline when he withdrew his hand. It was too dark outside to see anything else, only that brief fog, that mark of his touch. He returned to the washstand, stood a moment, looking into the mirror. He had his hand on his back again, could still feel the cool glass on his fingertips, looked at his tired face, the dark places under his eyes, feeling himself covered in dust from the dream, under his fingernails, crusting along his hairline, filling in the edges of a scar there, from a fight with another prospector over a claim, the wound purple at first, but thinning out and healing to white over time. Yet it seemed to have opened up again in the dream, gaped lividly at him now, and he lit the lamp, looking into the mirror once more, finding the wound suddenly healed. He washed his face with elbows drawn in, careful not to knock the lamp over, washing hardest at his eyes, his scar, at the places where he had seemed most begrimed. Stepping back to brush his sideburns and hair, covering the scar, making sure that he looked neat without any show of effort or care.

His expression was sombre, unpleasant. It was one he

knew well, that of the men of his family, all of those generals and colonels and admirals looking back at him through the reflection, observing him with disapproval. It was certain that he had failed, that he was a failure, every part of him a failure. The boy who had been unpredictable, disobedient, who had never settled as he should have done, taking his risks, coming up with his schemes, and losing every time, returning home with hands out in front of him, begging and desperate, because he was young and had nothing. Let that be a lesson to you, they'd said, let that be your comeuppance and serve to bring about a change in you. Yet he had not changed, and they could not forgive him for it. If only he had joined the army or navy, done something useful and befitting. If only he had been something more than this.

He looked back in the mirror, at his anger and shame, then made a point of throwing off the scowl, forcing a smile, pushing his shoulders down, saying cheerfully, "How do you do, how do you do, good morning." Saw his head nod, his hand reach out to take that of an imaginary person to his left, then doing the same to the right, until he was satisfied that it was convincing. In this way he set his mood, making sure as he dressed not to be distracted from it and pulled back into gloom. On the worst days, like today, when he felt he might slip easily, he did not join his wife for breakfast. He could not stand to face her disappointment in him, not hers on top of all the others, and went out into the morning, clutching his silver-tipped cane, swinging it a little as he whistled through his teeth, enough to show that he was in a pleasant mood, a man untroubled.

Going first to Hoffmeyer's on Plein Street, sharing a word or two with the tobacconist about the weather, the price of tobacco, shipments and delays, then asking after the man's daughter, who had recently married and moved to Stellenbosch. He bought a cigar, lighting it on the doorstep of the shop, walked on, nodding to passersby, stopping often to shake hands, clenching the cigar between his teeth, talking and laughing around it, or taking it in the fingers of the hand that held the cane, gesturing with them both. He asked always about families, including in-laws and cousins, remembering everyone, speaking of business only lightly, as an afterthought, yet all the while gathering information and using it to colour the map that he carried in his head.

The map had begun when first they arrived in Cape Town, knowing nothing then, no person, no street, no place but the dingy boarding house in which they stayed, and later, able to afford no better, a small Dutch cottage with crumbling walls, a wasp's nest in the thatch, and broken shutters that flaked green paint. No other decent person would have taken the cottage, there in Buitenkant Street beside a freedman and his wife who drank and screamed, and with the gallows opposite. Going out each day by himself, walking through the streets, learning every one of them, every alley, every plot, every dump, cutting the town into sections as he moved through it, and splicing them together in his mind. Over and over he went, the same streets, the same alleys and shops and dead ends, until the smallest details of the town were known to him. People began to recognise him, stopped being suspicious as he approached, began to return his greetings, taking the time to talk with him.

Emancipation was still being fought for then and he learnt when to make bold statements, quote Wilberforce, sign petitions. With others, he spoke of the danger of freeing so many people at once, sympathising at the loss of income, and later at the inadequate compensation being paid, not mentioning that he was getting rich off it. He said that he agreed with the need for the apprentice system, the need to teach them what it was to be independent, but agreed, too, with those amongst the Dutch inhabitants who were leaving the Cape, taking everything they had, including their slaves, trekking into the interior to start a new life, unhindered by British rules.

Approaching now that area near the gallows where he and Caroline had lived before. Many of the inhabitants he still knew, though it had been several years since they had moved to the house in the Heerengracht, with a bigger one coming, and a country cottage he was leasing from the governor. "Seven bedrooms and it's called a cottage!" he said to Caroline each time they went there. A while since their last visit, her sickness making the carriage ride too tiresome. But she had never seemed to be content there, disliking its tree gardens and gravel paths, complaining that there was no lawn, that the dust irritated her skin. Still, the shade was pleasant, and he liked to walk those paths when he could, remembering the woods where he had often been taken as a child, walking with his tutor who tried to show him ants and flowers and birds, quoting Milton, always Milton, no matter the occasion. Wanting none of that, not the words, the lessons, the company, wanting simply to lie down and stare up into the leaves, see the filtering of light, feeling that thing which was always inside him, that thing which was loud, loud, loud, coming to rest for a few moments. Doing the same at the country cottage when he could, when he was not called back to town on business, regularly having to leave Caroline there for days at a time, returning to find her as he had left her, on a chair, staring at the floor or out the window, greeting him without surprise or delight or even recognition.

In the old neighbourhood, he came upon those he had known as children and youths, some already with children of their own, and he had to stop as babies were brought out to him, that he might look at them, kiss them, give them a coin. Greeting him with handshakes, calling one another from backrooms to come and see him walk past, though he did it most days, always returning here, as though he had never left. Those first cold months he had known nobody, arriving at the start of winter, and every day it had stormed, raging, raging; sitting wet in the office after his walks, hoping for a patch of sun that he might go stand in, warm his feet and hands a little. A coldness that he could not get rid of, staying cold throughout the day, throughout the night, wishing for Caroline beside him in bed that he might turn to her and be held.

But already she had made it clear that she required a bed and room of her own, disgusted at what he had done, at where he had brought her. That small dank house, with only one bedroom, and beds hard to come by in the colony, so that he slept for the first year on a cot in the kitchen, while she had the brass frame they had brought with them.

trembling, starting to cry, allowing it to be more than tears, calling out, stricken and desperate. Wishing there was someone with her, someone who might have caught her, or helped her up now, pulling her towards them, their arms around her, holding her against their chest. Her mother, or September, or any other living being, that she might not feel the agony of this loneliness, of being utterly alone. Once before this feeling, this desperation, when her baby had been born, her little girl. Alone in the barn all those long hours of it, and the master coming to tell her to hurry up, can't you do it any faster? No one to help her or be with her, September already free and gone, never having known about the baby. Alone when her little girl was born dead, and alone gathering stones for the grave.

Wanting the baby to have something of September, wanting her to know him somehow, even in death. He had been of the Mohammedan faith, regularly meeting with others in the town, learning how to read, how to pray, had invited her to join the women in their lessons, but she had not been able to get away as he had. There was always something to be done, always the master calling for her. Yet she knew a little from what September had told her, and she prepared as best she could, gathering flowers, covering the small body in them, wrapping her in a scrap of sheet. Going out in the early morning, blood still coming from between her legs, making her way to the Mohammedan cemetery, finding a place at the edge, digging a hole with her hands, placing her little girl in it, then scooping the earth back into the hole, patting it into a small mound, laying stones from her apron on top. She had not brought enough, went about the cemetery gathering more. By now the town had begun to wake and she was afraid of being caught where she had no permission to be, hurrying back to the inn, to her chores, to grieving alone.

She put a hand up to wipe her tears, feeling a cut on her chin, another on her forehead, more on her arms and knuckles. Her dress torn now beyond mending and her injured leg damp with grazes. Ripping at the tatters of the hem, tearing off a length of fabric to tie around her ankle, the pain terrible as she bound it, pulling it tight. All the sorrows of her life with her now. Her baby dead in her arms, wondering what she had done wrong for her to have died. Thinking she had killed her with her grief at September leaving, at his not coming back. Grief at unkind words and hard work and nothing to call her own but her dead little girl. And now this, now this.

How long the night seemed as she sat holding her ankle, how long the wait for day, afraid to move, afraid of the pain that was vivid and clear and seemed to beat away everything else. Feeling it pulse out, sick with the force of it. And in the eventual morning light, removing the bandage, gasping as the pain spilled out, her ankle black and swollen, her legs, her hands and arms, red and yellow with wounds.

All morning hobbling, pulling herself along the rocks and sharp branches of mountain scrub, no sticks to be had, everything too short, too twisted. At times, resting under a bush or behind a rock, feeling the pain running up from her leg and surging through her, trying to lie still, to wait a while, but unable to come to rest. Knowing that it was coming, that she was being hunted down, someone was after her. Remembering the dead sailor, his grave before her eyes, then realising it could not have been his, that she had never been to it, had no idea where it was or what it looked like. These stones, this mound that stood out in her mind, this was the grave of her daughter. The two somehow becoming confused within her, and now she could not think what it was that was pursuing her, baby or man, or some creation between the two, comprising both grief and fear.

No path to go by, and she moved clumsily, sometimes turning back, having to find other routes when she could not make her way, everything being so much more difficult now in her pain. The trail she left was easy to track, and she expected at any moment to feel a hand on her shoulder, even stood still at times, waiting to hear the words, "I have you." Dreading it and wishing for it, for that relief.

In the heat of the late morning, flies found her, fed at her wounds, her eyes, her open mouth. No respite from the heat, the dips and rises of the mountain dry and savage. No water to be had. All the dew long since gone, the leaves hard and unyielding. The wind too, coming at her, on and on, never stopping, parching her into her bones. Sitting down, taking one of the tomatoes from her bundle, eating it for the moisture, cracks on her lips and at the edges of her mouth stinging from the acidity, but still eating the other one, the last one, and wanting more.

The day thickening, becoming unbearable. Continuing forward, feeling that she would never get away from Simonstown, which was still in view, the white cottages stark against the grey mountain slopes. She seemed to be walking in place, getting nowhere, stuck beside the same piercing bush, the same boiling rock.

Then she could smell it, could smell it before she reached it. A shelter of large boulders, a cave of sorts, into which she entered, water dripping at the back, along a wall of moss and ferns. Putting her hands on them, bringing her fingers to her mouth, pressing her face into the damp foliage, leaves in her nose, in her open mouth, tasting the earth, the soft green cold.

At last he reached Boom Street, came to the barber Destro, where every morning there was a queue of soldiers, of shopkeepers and tailors and carpenters, of convalescing officers from India, their skin yellow with illness, their voices hoarse. Destro welcomed him as he did each day, "Mr Kendrick, I will finish here and be with you right away."

No, said James in his usual fashion, he would wait his turn. He had a newspaper and he was happy to sit and read it, enjoy a little peace before he went to work, the men around him nodding and laughing. Someone brought him a cushioned chair from the back and he unfolded the paper, called a boy over, sent him to purchase a cup of coffee from the widow Erasmus next door, scanning the paper for advertisements of auctions and sales, properties for lease or purchase, few of them a surprise to him, but wanting to confirm what he already knew. Mostly he listened to the conversations around him, the map of the town filling out again as he heard mention of different places and people. They spoke of their wants and needs, of bargains they had come across, of what they would pay good money for and what they would not, sharing gossip about who was sure to be onto a good thing, or who was going bankrupt. By the time it was his turn in the chair he had added to the map, creating patterns and lines that linked the different areas. Everywhere was opportunity, and all of it his for the taking, the city waiting for him.

Leaning back, Destro's breath hot with cloves and something rank behind it. The razor gliding across his cheeks, hearing the rasp of it, feeling the mood, the expressions he had created before leaving the house, being scraped off, and he did not like the sensation, became impatient, wanted Destro to hurry up and be finished, set him free. Where he had been confident a moment before, confident of his map and his plans, he began now to doubt once more, each scrape of the blade making it worse. Holding himself taut, biting down so as not to wriggle, not to push the man from him, jump up and say, "For God's sake, have done and let me go." Clutching the arms of the chair, digging the nail of his right thumb into the wood, feeling it enter, digging it in again and again. He had had enough. This humiliation of being held down, of being kept here, being made weak and naked. Knowing with certainty that he was set for failure, that it was coming to him. That he had succeeded so far only by chance, and that misfortune was his curse, waiting for him.

Yet, he saw it so clearly, saw the opportunities, the places he had marked on the map, with plans for each of them. If only he had the money, if only he could conquer it all at once, take the whole town and make it his. But everything he had was tied up at present; in fact, he was overburdened, Caroline's money long since gone. A gift from her father upon her marriage, pin money for ribbons and lace, though it had been far more substantial than that, because he had not trusted James, had sat him down before the wedding, had said, "Swear you will take proper care of her, swear that she will not end up in the poorhouse," and he had sworn, had kept that vow. Was he to be blamed for venture after venture coming to nothing in the first months of their marriage, or for the fact that when he had confessed to her that they were penniless and desperate, she had handed all of her money to him without question, had said she trusted him to do with it what he would? And it had not been wasted, had it? After all, here they were, here they were! Yet how his old friends and family, Caroline most of all, looked at him. A man in trade, a merchant and insurer. "No, not that, surely not that," she had said when he told her. "Not trade, not the colonies."

It was with difficulty that he forced the smile to his face again, walking out of the barber shop with a strange step, wanting to march, to run, but holding himself back. The map, the damned map, blazing in his mind, pushing him forward, pushing him on into the streets, everything loud inside him, a bellow of triumph, of conquest, the city was his, all of it his. But always those dark eyes of hers on him, seeing his failure.

Tuesday
27th November 1838

Outside, at last. The violence of it like a tonic, the assault of the morning, the wind, the sea. Everything fresh and light after another long, blood-drenched night. Leah walking behind her, saying, "Slow down, miss, you must slow down." Swinging her arms, feeling them move against her sides, her upper arms tiring almost immediately, but pressing on, not wanting to stop, not this great rush of brilliant life.

Then Leah was holding her by one of those swinging arms, calling out something, pulling her away from the street. Just in front of them a carriage had been overturned by the wind. Horses screamed, struggling to right themselves, while passers-by rushed from both sides of the street. The driver was helped to his feet, the horses soon after, but the carriage lay on its side and had to be scrambled over to reach the door, so that it was a few minutes before the passengers were lifted out. There were only two of them, a lady whose name Caroline could not remember, though she knew her to be someone of importance, was certain she had been made to greet her during Sunday strolls in the Avenue. The lady's bonnet had been crushed in the fall, one of several green ostrich feathers coming loose. She held it in her hand, saying, "We might have been killed, we might have been killed." Then seeing that her slave apprentice girl had blood on her forehead, she said it louder, her alarm growing. "You see, we might very well have died, look at Katrijn, just look at her", taking out a handkerchief and holding it to the girl's forehead.

The girl had come out of the carriage already crying, had stood with her arms crossed, looking back at the fallen vehicle, the people around her. She put trembling fingers to her mouth, and Caroline had wanted to nudge Leah toward her, had wanted to know how it had been, to be tossed over in that way. But the girl had already seen the bloody handkerchief, grabbed it, letting out a wail, "I'm dead! I'm dead!" as her mistress was being led away to a nearby tearoom, still with the feather in her hand. Caroline heard the words wringing in the street, that cry of being dead, felt something warm within her, something like longing at this girl's panic, the whole thing a farce, a ridiculous entertainment. The girl kept pressing the handkerchief to her forehead, bringing it down to inspect the blood, pressing it to her again, then holding it out to those who surrounded her. Everyone craning to have a look, even Caroline, and listening as others gave their opinions, ready to tell anyone who would listen what they had seen of the accident and what the girl should do about the wound.

By now the carriage had been righted, the horses calmed. The driver made ready to return to the stables, and seven or eight loafers, men and boys hoping for a coin at the end, stood on either side of the vehicle, placing their hands on it in support against the wind. One of the men was unsteady on his feet, drunk and stinking of it. He had pushed himself to the front and was waving his free arm, shouting at the others as he ran alongside the carriage, "Like this, boys, follow me, keep it up, keep it up, lift your feet, lift them like this." But the trot of the horses was too much for him and he soon fell to the ground, tripping up the others. When they had passed, he tried to rise, fell again, calling after them, "That's it, boys, just like that, keep going," lying in the dust of the road like a man of leisure. This strange comedy before her, these fools and jesters, all of it wonderful and silly. Letting out a hard little explosive laugh, stifling another. Leah looking up at her with alarm, thinking her upset, saying, "We are going, miss, let's go, come on, we'll go."

Once more she was rushing on, her steps bouncing against the wind, and it was wonderful, wonderful to feel that freshness all around her, to see people going about their days, even to see them falling and bleeding, to see them drunk and idiotic, all of this life, all of this living. The wind great around them, lifting them up, propelling them on, wonderful to feel this force on her, not just the sound of it, that threatening harrowing sound, the endless vile rattling of doors and windows.

Odd in all this beauty to find herself thinking of James, imagining telling him about it over dinner. "You will never guess whose carriage has been blown over by the southeaster this time. That woman with the husband whose moustache is always unevenly waxed, you know the one. Oh, what is their name? You must know who I mean." Yet even as she thought it, she knew she would say nothing, knowing how he would react. Warning her of the dangers of leaving the house, saying that he had told her many times, many times, but that she did as she pleased, never listened to him, and why did he bother opening his mouth if he was to be ignored time and time again?

She lowered her head at once, slowed her pace, her eyes on the ground, on her footsteps. This was to be it, then, this was to be her morning. Everything light was gone, the bounce pushed down, pressed into some tight corner of her, and only dust now, this wide dusty street, strewn with brown paper, with corks, with rags and string, watching it pass under her skirt, feeling it through her soles, and somewhere, somewhere, a steady clink, clink, clink, moving in time with her footsteps, each sound sharp as a needle being driven through her, relentless as the rattling, the doors slamming, and she was in the house again, returned to that long red night.

The wind picked up, knocked her back a moment, blowing dust into her face. She felt grit in her eye, came to a stop, rubbing at it with her gloved finger, wiping away the tears. Once more Leah took hold of her, turned her from the wind, moved her until she was facing the wall of a nearby building, then blew gently into her eye, dabbing at it with a handkerchief. The irritation was gone, and she was blinking, blinking, smiling, saying, yes, she was all right now, no, she did not want to go back, she wanted to continue. Turning towards the street, ready to move on, and almost colliding with a chain gang of Mohammedan convicts. Here was the clink clink clink, these men in rags, their faces downturned, trudging with their bare feet. She met the glance of one of them as he passed, his wide yellow eyes, his hunted and broken expression, his dusty forehead and hair, this man who seemed to have resigned himself to his fate. She felt suddenly that she would like to know his name, to say it, to call it out to him, her head turning as he passed, her mouth opening but having nothing to call after him, only watching his shuffling form move off.

She heard still the clinking of the chains after he had gone, remembered other chains, the sound of them, remembering other eyes like his. James had gone back home for the second time, was collecting compensation money, for himself too – the price of Leah, who was being paid a wage now as a slave apprentice and who was afraid of spending it, each week asking Caroline to keep it safe for her. She kept the coins in an old purse at the back of her wardrobe, and from time to time, when Leah had particularly pleased her, she would call her to her bedroom, bring out the purse and they would sit on her bed, counting the money together. After they had added it all up, Caroline would frown. "That's not right," she'd say, and Leah would look worried, start counting the coins again. "But I haven't taken any, I swear. How much is missing?" Caroline would smile, go to her own purse, bringing out a coin and placing it in amongst the others. "There, now, that's better, isn't it?"

Promising her another coin one morning, sending her off on several errands, making them as complicated and far apart as she could so that she would be gone a long time. Putting on one of her oldest dresses, faded now and never worn out of doors, and a bonnet she had spent all the previous afternoon unpicking, removing the ribbons and flowers, pretending that she was tired of the design and wished to rework it. She drew a veil over her face, went out, trying as best she could to make herself invisible among the crowds that were gathering in the street and across the parade ground, everyone making their way to the gallows in the corner. She need not have gone to such trouble. There was to be a hanging and all manner of individual, from Mohammedans to Chinese and Jews and Dutch, had come to watch. No one looked at her.

The same longing she'd felt seeing the carriage fall, seeing the blood, the drunk, wanting to laugh, to laugh, to clutch hold of those around her in the crowd, share her excitement with them, to say, "I'm here, here I am, we're here and we are going to see something, be part of something."

But holding back, listening to the flurrying voices, people saying that this was proof enough of why emancipation could not happen all at once, that the four years of apprenticeship were necessary; they were clearly too savage to be allowed freedom suddenly, look at this slave who had killed his master, murdered him so brutally, this slave who was mad, quite mad, who did nothing but shriek and scream and groan, having lost the ability to form words. Yet there was no screaming when he was led out, only silence, and he seemed not to see the lunging crowd as they hissed and jeered at him, nor did he know where he was, and had to be told several times where to stand, what to do. He looked ancient, hunched up, a man already half-dead. There was nothing brutal left in him, only confusion and old age. It seemed vile now to kill him. Still, she watched his death, saw his quiet end, leaving immediately it was over, changing out of her costume, giving Leah her coin when she returned, telling no one about it, never a word to anyone. How could she admit why she had gone and what it was that she had wanted from it, and what she had got instead?

But here now were Mrs Cameron-Dow and her daughter, both holding their bonnets and laughing when they saw her. "Oh, this wind, we are quite blowing away, are we not?" said Mrs Cameron-Dow, and Miss Cameron-Dow added, "We are so looking forward to your party, Mrs Kendrick. We have just been to Chisholm's for a last fitting. A party of this kind requires new gowns, though Papa says he cannot understand this fuss over lace and frills and silly things."

Caroline felt everything lift then, forgetting the hanged man, the convict, her husband's shadow over the morning. Forgot it all, laughing too, saying that yes, men never did seem to understand these things, though she did not add that she had not bothered about a dress herself, because what did it matter after all, this talk of dresses, it didn't matter, only to be outside, to be outside and alive. She threw herself back into the street and the wind, letting it push her along, tripping forward, her hand on her hat.

"You must be on your way to the Infant School concert," Mrs Cameron-Dow called after her. "Come, let us walk together." Hooking her arm into Caroline's, halting her eager steps. "My word, this emancipation business is a to-do, isn't it? My Mary has been saying she will not stay a minute beyond midnight on Friday. Have you ever heard of such ingratitude? She says she and this man of hers are planning on getting baptised and then married and that she will have a home of her own. Mistress of her house, she says, and had the cheek to ask if I had any old curtains for her, knowing full well I have a set stored in the chest, but acting innocent as you please. Where will you possibly live, I said, because she has a room in the servants' quarters, you know, we have never made her sleep in the kitchen, and we always give her our old gowns, which she cannot very well expect if she is to abandon us, can she?"

"Mama is in quite a fury about it," said Miss Cameron-Dow. "We had not imagined this from her, and where are we to find a replacement with so little time? It is so tiresome having to train someone new, especially when Mary has been with us for my whole life and knows just how we like things done. You understand, I am sure, Mrs Kendrick. May I ask, will your girl be staying on with you?"

"Oh, we have not yet spoken of it, but she is so at home with us, she is quite happy, I am sure, and cannot think of leaving."

She looked behind her, saw Leah walking some distance away, saw her looking at pears in a basket, nodding to the seller, then Mrs Cameron-Dow was speaking again and Caroline cocked her head to hear better, the wind blowing the words away from her.

Grasping the back of his neck, feeling something quick and sharp roaring through him, just under the surface, a current running through him, all through his body, into his head, where it sat shivering. He knew this urgency, was often attacked by it, this uneasy roaring, roaring, with nowhere to go. Even at times like this, when the excitement of the wreck had left him tired, emptied out, even then that roaring coming to him, forcing its way through him, and there could be no rest, he must get up, he must be doing. But now he sat at his desk, the manifest before him. He had already been through the warehouse, matching his own ticks and crosses to those of Stone. Little had survived the wreck, and it was a pang, walking amongst the few sodden, salt-stained goods, knowing there should have been more, and feeling the loss of those items as strongly as if it had been he who had run the ship onto the rocks or tossed the cargo overboard.

Now he had to sit, to sit, to sit, looking at these losses, at item after item unaccounted for, columns of them, his crosses drawn with force, causing indentations that seemed to rise up under his fingertips, rough as calluses. Dropping the papers on his desk, disgusted by the feel of them, wiping his fingers on his trousers, up and down across his thighs, but the roughness staying with him, unwilling to be smoothed away, his fingertips becoming hot and red with the friction. All the while continuing to look at the papers, waiting for his mind to go hard, for the crosses to blur and recede, the pages to turn blank. Remembering the agony of sitting quietly, those years at school, first Winchester, like his father and brothers, then Woolwich for a while, and finally Haileybury as a last resort so that he might enter the East India Company as a drudging clerk, but being sent home from each in turn because he could not do it. Punished by the masters, the headmasters, by his tutors, his father, made to sit still, sit still, behave yourself, you must learn to behave, none of them ever understanding what was inside him. Running away when he could, running to the stables, the woods, to the market, the main street of any village nearby, always running, desperate, desperate, this thing inside him, this frenzy.

Stone knocked, opened the door. "You in?"

He slumped, rubbed his hand at the back of his neck and held it there. "Is it important?"

Stone shrugged.

"Then I'm not. Tell them to come back another time."

He looked again at the manifest, sick with it, sick, sick, the dreadful columns, the loathsome crosses, jumping up from his chair, going to the window, seeing some of his men standing around a large crate, talking, then going to his office door, opening it, watching Stone write at his desk. Stone looking up in inquiry. "Did you want something?"

"No, nothing."

Slamming the door, though he had not intended to. Pacing back and forth, looking out of the window once more. The men still talking. Tapping at the glass, but they did not hear him. Tapping louder, then banging with an open hand until the men looked up, seeing them mumble to one another, begin to slouch away from the crate, back to work. He sighed, paced to the door again, back to his desk, falling into the chair, pushing the manifest away from him, opening his drawers, looking through them, not for anything, only for something, something to occupy the urgency. Settling on a sheet of letter-headed paper, putting the date in the righthand corner, on the next line writing "Dear", then not knowing what should follow, flicking the pen between his fingers, dipping it into the ink again, writing slowly, deliberately, "FATHER."

He paused, watching the ink well up in the nib of the pen, drip onto the page, spread as it soaked into the paper, covering the last two letters of the word. He began a new line: "If only..." Scratched it out. Began another: "I would have wished..." Scratched that out too, then took the paper and drew a large X across it. His father had been dead five years. There was nothing to say now. He tore the paper in half, then half again, taking the pieces between his hands, crushing them into a ball and throwing them into the wastepaper basket. But still that current running through him. He'd not stay here, he couldn't, he must do something, must conquer this feeling, bring himself to exhaustion somehow. Not this roaring, roaring of his mind, his body, this empty, tired, hopeless roaring.

Getting up, taking his top hat and cane from the stand, opening the door, not looking at Stone, saying only, "I'll be out for a while."

"The manifest?"

"Yes, yes, all fine. It's on my desk. You can set up the auction."

But he was bitter, frustrated, and what to be done about it, what to be done? Trying to hold himself upright, trying not to burst into a sprint, run furiously down the road. Something keeping him from that; his father's hand on the back of his neck, holding him there, a claw, a vice, and there was Hugo on the other side, allowed to walk freely, no reprimanding hand near him. Walking along the dirty docks at Bristol, his father having business to attend to, and them accompanying him, being shown off, "Yes, Hugo will be joining his brother at Winchester soon, no, this is the middle one, James, no, he is at home at present," the claw clenching and releasing as he spoke.

James looked around, away, towards the boats and ships in the water, sailors and barrels and crates, seagulls flying low, the sky grey with winter cold, and there, further along the harbour wall, a row of negroes was standing, half naked, emaciated, burrowing against one another for warmth. James tugged at his father's jacket, "Who are they, Father, who are those people?", was told they had been meant for sale, but slaves could no longer be sold, so they were being confiscated and would be given out as servants. "Not sold?" he'd asked. No, not sold. Looking across at the naked bodies, the big ships, the filthy water, saying more to himself than to his father, "But it's terrible." And being given a florin by the gentleman to whom his father had been speaking, a member of parliament, who said, "We need more men like you, young chap, to ease the troubles of the world." Later displaying the florin for Hugo to see across the table as they dined, holding it out to him, then snatching it back just as he reached for it, because Hugo was not the future as he was and did not deserve a reward. Telling himself this story often, that he was special, had been selected for greatness, yet all the time knowing the truth of it; that what he had meant when he spoke was that it was terrible the negroes were not to be sold, that the opportunity had been lost.

In the street outside the warehouse he stopped, adjusted his top hat, felt in his pockets for a cigar. Across the way stood a group of six men, their clothes worn and mismatched, their faces hard. They nudged one another as he came out, all of them looking at him, taking an expectant step in his direction. He returned the cigar to his pocket, lifted his cane, walking away from them with brisk steps. He did not want to talk to anyone, wanted to be left alone. But they came after him, matching his pace, their heels clipping in time with his own, whispering to one another, "It's him, I tell you", "Say something", until one of them called his name, too loud for him to ignore. Turning towards them, their sunburnt faces, their unkempt stubble, seeing them remove their caps and hats, hold them at their stomachs.

"What do you want?"

"We're from the ship…" one of them said, stopping uncertainly, another coming forward, "The Dunlop, sir, the one what sank."

"And what is that to me?"

"Sir, you see, sir, we've lost everything."

He gestured towards the warehouse with the tip of his cane, frustrated, wanting to get on. "My deputy can inform you of what, if any, personal items have been found. Good day."

Turning to go then, but one of the men, darting forward,

reached out a hand to him. "Begging your pardon, sir, if you please, you see, thank you, sir, but it's more than that. We've lost everything, you see, and we're poor men, sir, with nothing, just the bit we'd saved for the journey, and we were on our way to Australia because they say there's land there to be had and anyone can make himself rich. Fred's cousin –" The man nudged one of his neighbours, "Tell him, tell him what your cousin said."

James raised his cane. "Gentlemen, I am a busy man."

"Yes, sir, the point is, sir—"

"No, I will tell you the point. I have told you that you must speak to my deputy. What's more, there has already been a subscription put up for the survivors, to which I have given generously. More than that I cannot do, other than to offer you some advice. You act as though you are stranded here, as though all hope is lost, but look about you, a man can make himself just as rich here as he can elsewhere, more so, if he only cares to put in the effort."

"Yes, sir, but..."

He shook his head, waved them off, then withdrew his cigar once more, placed it in his mouth without bothering to light it, walking on with it dangling there, the taste an abundance on his lips.

There were not enough seats at the Infant School concert, but one had been kept aside for her in the front row, beside the governor's wife and other people of importance whose names topped the list of subscribers. The room was overcrowded, windows closed against the wind, a profusion of hats and feathers, of waving hands and excited greetings, making it stifling, and she stood still upon entering, trying to catch her breath. Someone took her arm, led her to her seat, gave her a cushion to make her comfortable, and then they were there, all the people of the room it seemed, one after another coming up to her, asking after her health, after James, the party, whether it was still to occur, weren't they afraid of the unrest? Mrs Sellars saying she wouldn't be able to attend, not the way things were, she hoped Caroline would understand, but she couldn't take the risk, calling her girl over, telling her to hold up the baby, little Charles, hold him up and let Mrs Kendrick see, look at those little hands and the sweet little nose, you may hold him, you know, but Caroline shook her head.

Then Mrs Buxton was tapping the dais and everyone took their seats, listening as they were welcomed and told of their Christian duty to these poor souls, to educate them and prepare them for a future in which they could work as fine servants anyone would be proud to have in their employ. The Reverend Johnson spoke next, slowly, so slowly, hard to understand after the onset of palsy some months before, the words lumpen, struggling, everyone waiting for him to reach the end of his sentence, please God, let him get to the end, the room hushed waiting for it, and then an intake of breath, a frustrated waiting as he began another, and another, until at last he finished and the children were being marched out in their clean, patched clothes, their hair wet and combed back, the girls too, with tiny little buns, even those with barely any hair at all, all manner of races and colours, made to stand in rows, told to remove their hands from their pockets, from in front of their mouths, from crying eyes, and look here, look at me, the teacher said, pointing to her mouth then to theirs, miming for them to smile widely, and ready now, all together, one two three, their arms around one another's shoulders, singing, "We love one another, as children ought to do."

There was more to sit through after that. More songs, chanting of poems, Bible verses. One boy was made to wear a sheet wrapped around him, a crown of leaves in his hair, and recite an extract in Latin from the Gallic Wars. His eyes wandered around the room as he lost his place, stumbled, went silent, before mumbling it all again under his breath until he found where he had stopped and could begin out loud once more. She didn't know Latin, didn't know what he was saying, wondered whether he had any idea himself. Then lady Buxton was back, speaking of the importance of subscriptions to continue the good work, especially now that there would be so many coming to the town, so many in need of improvement, needing to learn how to live as Christians, with dignity and discipline.

The cushion was uncomfortable at Caroline's back, her neck and shoulders hurting, the seat hard beneath her. She shifted a little, felt the cushion fall, and Mr Graham behind her bent down, picked it up, was passing it back, having to smile at him, whisper her thanks, keeping the smile for the governor's wife who was saying for the tenth time, Aren't they adorable, aren't they simply delightful, look at that little one over there. Nodding again, smiling again. She had lost the morning's thrill, felt only the weight of the room, these whispers, these smiles, the aching weight of it. The governor's wife once more tapping her on her forearm with her fan and she wanted to snap at her, say, I have seen them, I have seen them all, every one of them! But she was not pointing at the children now, was indicating the back of the room with her fan and her smile.

It was James. James leaning against the wall beside the doorway, standing amongst the other men who had come too late for seats. James watching the children, the recitals, not looking at her at all. She felt a jolt of sickness, knew he must have seen her, must have been watching her, could feel it, of course he had been, he must have been, though he kept his eyes away now, even when she gave a little cough of fright, clearing the nausea burning in her throat, even then he didn't look towards her. Wanted to jump up, go to him, apologise for this, for being here, in this place, without him, though he had known she was coming, she had asked him, had said for days that there was to be this concert and that she was expected to attend, because of the subscription. It is you who paid it, she could have said, you who paid it and put my name to it, you who wanted to see it in the papers, it is you who put me here. You cannot blame me for this.

Waiting for something, a glance, a movement, something

to connect them. But the only movement was away from her, towards the window, turning his head to look out into the hot noon, continuing to lean as he had done in those early days when she had first begun to know him, just back from America where he had experienced some or other ill fortune, some bad luck that had sent him home, and he leaned in this way at every party, every ball, his expression painful, imploring. Coming up to her once at Sir Edward's, saying abruptly, "Miss Caroline, your dress is as blue as the skies of North Carolina," her mother standing beside her, Lady Brentworth and Mrs Dawlish as well. The three of them laughing with delight, calling him a poet, a brooding Shelley or Byron, pressing him to say something further, but he returned to the wall, to his silence.

Later going to him, to where he had been looking at a painting for the better part of an hour, clenching and unclenching his fists, shifting up and down on his feet. Saying his name, and he turned with a start, his hand brushing against the folds of her dress. He did not withdraw it, kept it there though it trembled, made her dress tremble along with it, some energy in him, luminous and alive, and she thought it was for her, because of her nearness. Asking him what he saw in the painting, turning with him towards it, and remembering little of what he said, only the gentle glow of the landscape's horizon, his hand lifting, still trembling, pointing out the mountain, saying something about mines and quarries, about rocks and minerals, but she saw none of that, watching instead his trembling fingers, the soft, dark hairs.

Now the governor's wife was standing, all around chairs

were creaking, scraping against the floor, and words of congratulations were being spoken, she too was saying them, being pulled forward to smile at the children, the teachers, to shake the hand of the boy in the toga, to pat the cheeks of the little ones. To say, yes she was quite well now, certainly well enough to help serve the tea, allowing herself to be put to work, arranging cakes and sandwiches at the trestle table in the other room, saying, yes, wasn't it lovely, oh it had warmed her heart, then James was there, standing across from her, saying, "A triumph, Mrs Buxton, quite the triumph."

Only then did he look at her, and she was ready for him, holding a cup and saucer, but his eyes, there was something in them of that trembling luminosity she had seen beside the painting, and it frightened her, made her draw back, because she knew she did not understand it, had never understood it, had been wrong, blind and wrong. Turning from him, offering the cup of tea to Mr Douglas instead, saying, "Here you are, ready and waiting just for you. Do you take sugar?" with a breathy laugh, and "oh, where are the sugar tongs?" which had disappeared again, looking for them, laughing with Mr Douglas, not daring to look up, not wanting to see… and there they were, the tongs, beside the teapot, helping Mr Douglas to his lumps, having to look up then, but her eyes remaining firmly on the teacup. Still, she could see that James had gone. Feeling no relief at that, only pain, for not having spoken to him, for him not having spoken to her, and more than that, so much more than that, heavier than the weight of the room, the smiles and nods, there was the burden of longing for something that she knew he could not give her and which she herself could not name.

He did not reach the Commercial Exchange until late afternoon, had spent the day striding through the streets, stopping from time to time to talk, to listen, then rushing on again, saying, "Forgive me, I am late for an appointment, I have some place to be," all the while that current moving within him, pushing him forward, searching for something, feeling the need within him for a conclusion, some great moment of arrival and release. If only he could tell someone about it, this tiring, thrilling, frightening thing. In St George's Street he had passed the Infant School, heard the singing coming from inside, remembered that Caroline would be there and he entered without thought, wanting to go to her, to clasp her hands, her forearms, pull her to his chest as he had done in the past, and have her look back at him as she used to, with bright eyes, saying, yes, he could do anything, yes, it was all possible, yes, she believed he would succeed. Wanting to take her by the hand, pull her back out into the streets, move through them, showing her the map, his plans, all the visions and hopes for the city that lived frantic inside him. Seeing her nodding to the governor's wife in the front row, the tired expression on her face, her downcast eyes, he was reminded of what he had forgotten, that there was too much between them, a wide and barren expanse they could not cross.

The Exchange was empty at this late hour, most of the businessmen having left already or settled in for the evening at the Masonic Lodge, and he walked without interruption towards the rooms he was leasing, tapping his cane loudly on the stone floor. Stopping at the sight of a brass and mahogany sign above the entrance to the rooms: First Colonial Bank.

Taking the cigar out of his mouth, swearing loudly, then walking into the first of the three rooms and finding it empty but for a couple of workers papering the walls. They looked up as he entered, greeting him with a mumbled "Sir"

"Where is O'Brian?"

One of the men shrugged, the other said that O'Brian had left for lunch some hours ago and had not yet returned.

"For God's sake, take that sign down. I told him it was not to go up until Friday for the unveiling. Is this Friday? Tell me, is this Friday?"

They put down their brushes, "No, sir, no", making their way towards the entrance.

"And mind you be careful with it. Signs like that cost a pretty penny I can tell you, a fortune, a damn fortune, and far more than either of you would ever have fetched."

"Yes, sir," said the one who had been silent before, then "Excuse me, sir" as he pushed past with a ladder.

The room smelled of glue, felt hot and uncomfortably small. James took off his top hat, held it carefully to keep it away from the walls, walked across the length of the room, taking large steps, counting them out loud, then did the same across the breadth, unable to remember what the measurements were meant to have been, but the room was smaller, certainly smaller, of that he was sure.

The men came back in, staggering under the weight of the sign, asking where to put it, and he pointed to a wall. They leaned it there, stood looking at him, their breaths hot, patient, as the room shrank even further. He was being crushed by those breaths, the smell of glue, by the walls pushing at him, pressing into his back, his thighs, coming in towards his face. "Go, just go," he said. "I'll talk to O'Brian when he reappears." The men ducked and bowed. "Thank you, sir, thank you."

He walked over to a window, flung it open, took a deep breath. "For God's sake, for God's sake," composing himself, then turned back to face the room. The sign stood beside him, marked with glue and dust from where the men had touched it. He wiped at the smudges irritably with his gloved hand, but they would not come off, and he took out a handkerchief, spat on it, getting down on his haunches and rubbing, the glue curling, coming off in sticky gobs. Through the window he could hear people passing by across the Grand Parade as he worked, snatches of conversations reaching him.

"All earthenware, you say?"

"Some glass too, I think. Decanters and goblets, from what I hear."

"Should sell well."

These words, this conversation in particular, the mundane nature of it, caught at him. The current which had been coursing through him all day suddenly stopped, and he was at once stagnant. Standing up, returning his handkerchief to his pocket, though there remained glue on the sign. What was it worth, all of this, these parties, these schemes, the silver topped cane, the mahogany and brass? Everything frantic and pointless, always the same, the same, nothing new. Futile activities, repetition of words and phrases and all of it taking so much time, so much energy. All one ended up with was mistake after mistake. What hideous impulse had made him lease these precise rooms, knowing they stood opposite the Cape of Good Hope Bank, knowing the arrogance of that decision? It was part of the ridiculous show of it. Of making himself something, of being seen. This great audacity had chosen the rooms for the bank just as it had chosen this venue to hold the party. Here, of all places, where subscription balls and concerts were held, this massive building, with its Grecian façade, so that it stood on the parade like a temple to wealth and commerce. Here, in all this space, he chose to show himself to everyone. The expense of it, the expense. Of hiring tables and chairs. Food, and the military band, and a small orchestra of slave apprentices for when the military band grew tired. All of this expense and madness, because he had had a vision of himself, like some god in his temple, leading everybody to the doors of his bank, inviting them in to worship him. He had seen it with such clarity, had known for certain that it was coming.

But he'd been mistaken, had been wrong, horribly wrong. The map, the plans, the colours and patterns, they were all false. There was nothing and he would fail again. He wished he could sit down. Felt tired, exhausted, felt that a great emptiness had come to him, all of him empty, and his mind, those maps and visions, erased. Everything colourless and grey, he too, his whole self gone, everything had slipped away from him.

FIRST OF DECEMBER

Watching from the ravine above Muizenberg since morning, seeing the small boats, the men even smaller, moving across the bay in chase of the blackfish. Three boats, each with harpoons that they flung and missed, flung and missed, until striking the great hide and holding the rope fast as they struck again and again, the blackfish thrashing, trying to dive away from them. Hours it seemed to take, this process of tiring the beast out, back and forward through the water, over and over, the water pink where it went, and its tail writhing, the head arching all the way up, then crashing down, but the men always nearby, not letting go.

At last, it had given up, scores of others joining the whalers, wading out, taking hold of the ropes and slowly dragging it in to shore. The beach full of spectators, people running down from their small cottages at the edge of the mountain, with hacksaws and blades, pails and basins, staggering under tubs that took two or three men to carry. Children racing to the water, shrieking, running back to their mothers' aprons. Seagulls circling, coming closer, landing on the creature where it lay on its side, screeching and pecking as men panted in the shallows. Seals, too, playing nearby, or floating with one flipper up, lazy in the afternoon heat. The blackfish shuddering, thrashing its tail, and then nothing.

All this time waiting for them to leave, nervous of going down to the beach with so many people around. She had not imagined the killing would take so long, and still the butchering to be done. No longer able to hold back her hunger, though she had tried all day, digging for roots where she could, but those she found were bitter and made her mouth feel chalky, her tongue and cheeks dry. No other option now but to continue with her slow descent, going carefully, letting the hurt of her ankle build into a rhythm, getting used to it, and only pausing when the rhythm broke and the pain jolted her.

Down below, the blackfish was being worked on, bits of it being carried away, the whole changing shape and colour as she moved closer, coming down to the bottom of the ravine and stepping onto the wagon road. Gaping areas of flesh and blubber stood out where there had been black skin before, water red all around it, and everyone moving in it touched by that red too.

Waiting to make sure nobody was passing on the road, crossing as quickly as she could, then following a sandy path through dune grasses down to the beach. Not going towards the creature, moving instead away from the commotion, towards the far end of the shore where there were rockpools, her ankle lurching across the uneven sand.

Dusk already, the water dark, yet silvering into ripples as she sat down to the sharpness of salt on her grazed leg. Hunching forward, rubbing where it stung, her knuckles stinging now, but glad of it, glad of this change from heat and hunger and pain. She moved a little, leaning further forward, searching for mussels where they grew at the base of the rocks, feeling their sharp edges. Her fingers slipping, getting cut as she pulled at them. But continuing, seeking out the largest ones, loosening them, some of them coming away in clutches, so that she had handfuls of blue-black that clacked and grated. Knowing not to try prying them apart, knowing they would hold themselves closed, that her hands did not have the strength to open them. September had shown her how to do it, fishing a stone out of the water, placing the mussels on the rock beside her where green seaweed had dried crackly in the day's heat, taking the stone and smashing the shells, picking out the innards and dropping them into her mouth. Doing this sometimes when they could get away for an hour or two on a Sunday, going down to the small beach near the inn and collecting mussels, eating some of them fresh like this, not for the taste but to be doing it together, laughing at him when he missed a shell, hit his hand instead. Putting the rest in her apron, carrying them to a sheltered spot and building a small fire, placing them on rocks beside it, waiting until the heat cooked them open, then picking them up with the tips of their fingers, the shells too hot, dropping them often, picking them up again, blowing the heat and sand away, and using a twig to poke out the small orange heart inside, eating and eating until they had had their fill. Afterwards, his mouth on hers, tasting of the sea, and of that moment, of everything good and warm.

Going out into the evening, the wind fierce across the exposed flatness of the Grand Parade. Labourers trudging home after work, fruit sellers and watercarriers packing up their wares, walking heavily with their baskets and urns. Messenger boys gathered at the bottom of the steps of the Exchange, playing games with dirty cards, worn to transparency with use. He stood at the top of the steps, watched them throw down their winning hands, heard their calls to one another. It seemed a long way to where they were, a long way to reach the cobbled parade grounds, to cross that windy expanse, and then to go where? Once more out into the streets, his feet tired and burning? Or home, to what? To sit sullen and miserable with Caroline? To sit with her hatred filling the room, to have that loathing wrap around him, enter him, choke him into a rage. Sharp the memory of the early months of their marriage, her hair loose, soft against his skin, and her yielding body, her smooth hands on him. All of her loving him, wanting him. But none of that now. None of that. Knowing what he was to her, knowing that she saw the truth of him, that he was petty and worthless and insignificant, that she had every reason not to love him.

Then someone was greeting him, saying his name. Looking around, seeing Richard Percy coming up the steps, raising his hat, wishing him a good evening. James returned the greeting, bringing his fingers up to his hat brim, lifting it a little, then went back to watching the boys and their game, their devastating losses, their exuberant wins. One of the boys slapped down a card, the others crying out as he jumped up, did a little jig, his laugh showing the brown stains of his teeth. James clenched his jaw at the spectacle, his nail pressing into the hard wood of his cane, trying to dig into it, grip onto something, pressing, pressing, making no headway, and then he was remembering, some spark, some moment from the barber's chair, and he turned, called, "Wait!", running up the steps, catching Percy at the entrance and saying, "You have land to sell, I believe, out there near Rondebosch, is that correct?"

"My word, news travels fast in these backwaters." He gestured up towards the Heerengracht. "I've only just been to Fairbairn to enquire about advertising in the Commercial Advertiser."

James shifted his cigar to the hand with the cane, placed the empty hand on Percy's shoulder. "No, no, no, a waste of money, my friend. Haven't I told you to come to me first whenever you have anything of interest?"

"But I didn't think it could be of interest to you, not when you've only just bought that place in New Street, and I know you have another venture soon to be announced," nodding towards the entrance to the Exchange. "Besides, how many houses does a man need, with not even a child to fill the empty rooms? Come, come, you must leave something for us family men, you know."

The mention of his childlessness stung, but he pushed that hurt out of himself, thrust it towards Caroline, for this and for everything, for all he had had to organise on his own, the houses, the deals, this party, this stupid party, with no help from her, no arrangements for the linen, or finetuning the menu, no conversing with cooks and suppliers, no keeping track of invitations and responses. None of that, and now this too, public and contemptible, of being without a son, or a daughter even. Yes, even that she denied him. But he made himself laugh, said, "Oh, there's time enough for all that. Now, what size are we talking?"

"Fifty erven, or thereabouts."

"Good, good. Listen, Percy, tomorrow, early, as soon as I can, I will ride out and have a look. It's for me, you understand? Don't sell to anyone else until we have spoken, will you agree to that?"

He looked at James's gesturing arms, then out across the Parade, twisting his mouth as he thought. "Well, all right, but only until tomorrow afternoon. That's fair, I'd say, wouldn't you?"

"Yes, yes. That's fair, that's all I ask."

No longer feeling tired, not wanting to stay there at the top of the steps, looking down at washerwomen moving slowly with baskets of clothing and linen on their heads for ironing into the night. Not wanting to see the boys playing their foolish games, or the two men struggling past with a large fish between them. Once more this heave of energy within him, a force driving him out so that he must be moving. Dashing down the steps, out into the filth and chaos, into the dirt and stink, following the people as they made their way to their cellar homes, their attic rooms, their shacks and tumbling cottages. To the slums where the poorest and most desperate lived.

Here the windows were boarded up with scraps of wood or yellowing pages. All throughout the unpaved alleys, at the doorsteps, were piles of human excrement, of rancid meat and old bones, the carcasses of animals. Chickens and pigs wandered amongst it, feeding on dead dogs, on human filth. Despite the season, despite the wind, everything damp, the eaves dripping, the walls crumbling and bubbling, brown with running water. Puddles of green filling the street. Toddlers played in it, dogs drank from it, people splashed through it. James walked amongst that chaos, feeling no disgust, no horror. This was the map being drawn, this was what he would do with the land. Construct quickly, cheaply, using their own labour to build the homes the newly liberated would need. So fierce was the urgency in him that he did not go home as he had planned, went instead via Snaakoog Alley, where he paid a certain woman to see what his excitement could do.

The sun had set behind the mountain, yet she could see to the other side of the shore where fires had been lit, many of them, easily thirty or more, brightening that section of the beach so that the outline of the changing blackfish was clear in the water, as was the rush of movement all around it. The evening cooling, and she shivered a little in her damp dress, coming away from the rockpools, back onto the sand. Wind blew the smell of cooking meat to her, carried the sound of voices. She had not meant to go towards them, had meant to stay in her corner of the beach, but seemed to be stepping closer to the smell of food, until she could feel the heat of all those flames on her cheeks, could taste the meat, almost sick with need of it.

Blood too, everywhere blood, all over the sand, the people, the objects that lay around, and behind that the thick, fishy smell of fat being rendered into oil, giant pots of it cooking down on fires all around. Though they had been at it for hours, there was more to come, still the enormous shape of the creature hulking in the shallows, its great eye flickering in the light of the fires, seeming almost alive, lying there watching her, aware all the while of its own slow and painful disintegration.

But she had come too close, was standing in the way, a man pulling a hunk of blubber and skin on a giant hook, dragging it through the sand, pushed past her, smearing grease and blood over her, "Have you no sense, girl?" She said sorry, moved out of his way, stepping in front of another man now, this one carrying a smaller amount in his arms, his face blackened with smoke and sweat. She could not see where to go, everywhere around her suddenly active and full. A woman passing nearby, with a pail of blood-sodden meat in each hand, paused with a grunt to drop them in the sand a moment, wiping a dirty forearm across her sweating face. "Come, make yourself useful," pointing to one of the pails and jerking her head in the direction of the fires. Leading her up the beach, past several fires where large pots of blubber were being boiled down. Around the fires people sat on what appeared to be the trunks of strangely-formed trees. Wondering where they had come from; no such trees on the mountain or anywhere she had seen. Putting out a hand to touch them as she passed, and even then unable to place the texture, not until the woman came and took the pail from her and said, "Bone." Only then understanding that they were the remains of previous killings, scattered and loose across the beach, bleached white as any other bone might be, but massive and ghastly in the firelight.

"Sit," said the woman, gesturing with her chin to a group of about twenty men and women, some on bones, others on skins and blankets, or the bare sand. Children among them, watching the goings-on with sleepy eyes.

"Here, sit here," the woman said, pointing to one of the bones. "Shift up, Apoolis, let the girl sit."

The man looked up, smiling toothlessly, sliding across a little, those beside him moving along too. Joining them shyly, suddenly aware of her torn clothes, her bandaged foot, the wounds all over her body. The toothless man smiled again, handed her a bottle, she took it, lifted it to her nose. Nearby, several people had started dancing, everyone at the fire beginning to call and laugh and clap. The toothless man asked if she wanted to dance, she shook her head, and he laughed, rising to do a little shuffling step where he stood, then sat down again, putting out his hand for the bottle and taking a large sip.

The smell, the sounds, reminding her of home, of the inn and the breath of the sailors as she served them, as they pulled her onto their laps, pressed her against walls. Their hands broad and firm, holding her tight. From time to time holding too tight, not letting go, wanting more from her and taking it, sometimes giving her money afterwards. Those few dirty coins, hating them, but keeping them. Hiding them away for her freedom, if that ever came, so much confusion about it, about what freedom meant and when it was to be, and everyone saying something different about how many years were left and what the rules of apprenticeship were, so that she didn't know, was never sure what to believe, the master unreliable and others as confused as she was. Gathering those coins when September left, thinking nothing of her freedom then, taking them and holding them out to him. He hadn't wanted them, told her to keep them, she'd need them for herself, but she had put them in his pack anyway, that he might eat along the way, have something, maybe a place to sleep when he got to Cape Town. Perhaps believing the money would somehow bring him back faster.

Across from her, two women cut bits off a slab of meat, placing them on skewers made from gathered twigs, then handing them to others who held them near the flames, cooking them black, before passing them around the group.

She sat quietly, watching, and the woman who had spoken to her before said, "Eat, eat, there's more than enough," as the man with the gums handed her a skewer. "Careful, it's hot, go slowly, don't forget to blow," he said, spitting a little as he spoke. It must have been a joke because everyone was laughing then and miming blowing and wiping spit off their faces. She laughed too, let herself laugh at this thing she didn't understand, because it felt good to be part of it, to be with people again.

Going to the market once a week, talking with the ladies there, or the woman who did the washing who would stand for a while with her in the yard, sharing her news, always something to tell because she went around all the houses and knew everything that was going on in the town. Telling a story once about the admiral's linen, which she couldn't remember now, only the laughter, laughing so hard that September had come running all the way from the vegetable patch to scold them, saying the master would be angry and would punish them, he was already in a foul mood that day and they mustn't provoke him, but still they had laughed, doubled over, going around to the back of the barn to laugh some more.

Bringing the hot greasy meat to her mouth, feeling it almost at once to be too rich, her stomach squirming, throat filling with slime from the mussels before. All eyes on her, continuing to mime blowing, their lips puckered as they cheered and clapped. She swallowed hard, then blew on the skewer, nodding at everyone, letting them see that she was following along, playing her part. Soon the nausea passed enough that she could take a bite, the meat warm and good. Smiling, holding up the skewer, then taking another bite, and another, hardly chewing, getting through it all until there was no more, and she was gnawing at the bits of meat that still clung to it. Someone handed her another, fresh from the fire, and she was blowing again, blowing and swallowing, feeling how everything within her that had been sharp and on edge had been muted and calmed.

Tired now, sweating a little from the fires, the food. Tired and heavy, unable to keep her head up. Moving aside, away from the noise, finding herself a sheltered wall of bone, putting her head on the sand, making a pillow of it. Movement all about her, and here, within the sand at her head, that movement in soft scratching echo. Motion and motion, gentle in her ear. That soft tickle of life and death, of blood and meat, of people dancing, moving, laughing, all of this around her, soothing her to sleep beside the bones on the warm sand.

Wednesday
28th November 1838

The streets quiet at that hour, only a few huddled forms sleeping in doorways, or making their way to work. Clattering into that emptiness, his horse's hooves echoing off the fronts of the silent houses, disturbing the sleepers inside. But he could not think of sleeping, had not slept himself, maddened by the energy that sat inside him, dashing forward, the glow of the low moon behind him, the houses becoming squatter, more run down, the trees fewer as he moved further and further towards the dark outer reaches of the town.

He had brought no lantern, thinking he would find his way easily enough. But twice the horse had stumbled in the increasingly potholed road. He began to regret his decision, thinking with anger that it might be necessary to dismount, wait for the sun to rise, yet he could not stop, not when so much was waiting. Pressing on into the dark, only slowing a little, peering into the dirt and shadows, trying to decipher the route, then coming with surprise upon a light blinking ahead of him. Slowing further, bringing the horse to a stop as they approached the mass of dark shapes around a lantern; a wagon, with a team of sixteen oxen, all standing, asleep on their feet, the driver asleep too, hunched forward on his seat, looking as though he might fall at any moment. Behind the wagon, a small flock of drowsing sheep, their shepherd, a young Hottentot boy, asleep on the ground beside them, wrapped in a hide. And two further wagons, drivers asleep as well, with Hottentot servants lying on top of bags of wheat, piles of vegetables and fruit, all of them tired from the journey from the interior.

"Hello there, you there, hello, wake up, will you! Wake

up, you're taking up the whole damned road!" he called, and the first driver sat up, looked at James crossly. He didn't say a word, took his long whip and cracked it three times, reaching all the way to the front pair of oxen. The sound was loud as gunfire and the oxen started awake, began lumbering forward. The boy woke as well, jumping up, rubbing his eyes, calling to the sheep, taking a switch to the stragglers as they stumbled to their feet, bleating nervously. Soon the whole procession was moving, and James could hear the slow turning of wheels, the tired tread of oxen. They did not make way for him, forcing him to move his horse to the side of the road, where it snorted and shook its head, disliking the soft sand, unwilling to proceed.

"Come on, come on!" he called, though they made no greater show of haste, the boy smiling at him, the others watching him with sleep-narrowed eyes. There rose the smell of fresh-trampled soil as they passed, of animals' clean droppings, the crisp headiness of vegetables, carrots and cauliflowers, mounds of them, turnips and beetroot, sweet potatoes, bags of onions. He had left home without eating, had not had the patience even for a cup of coffee, not wanting to rouse the girl and have to wait for her to build a fire, heat the water. Keen now to bend down and grab a carrot or two, eat them raw in the saddle, but daylight was starting silver behind the distant mountains, and the wagons had passed at last, he was moving again, feeling the rhythm of the horse beneath him, pressing on into the dawn with that gnawing feeling in his stomach that was not quite hunger.

Hearing him rise early, footfalls heavy from his riding boots. In her half-sleep, thinking him on his way to her, turning towards the door in expectation of him coming to lie beside her, his stubble on her neck, speaking low in her ear to wake up, to get dressed and come riding with him. Readying herself for it, a smile waiting for him. But he was passing the room, clattering down the stairs, making no attempt to be quiet, knocking something over, pulling the front door to, opening it again almost immediately, stomping around, going out again. And she was awake, fully awake, remembering where she was, and when. Turning onto her back, looking up towards the ceiling, the red, oppressive room, and imagining herself out of it, away from this into the smell of hay and stables, riding across pastureland, the sky broad above, softening into the green and gold of hills and fields. Easily spending a few hours that way, coming back flushed and tired to join her family for tea, eating first a piece of seed cake and then bread and butter, slice after slice of it until her mother would say, "Really, my dear, that is quite enough."

A different person then, painful to remember now how she had stood up when James had come calling, all the way from London, sitting stiffly because he knew what was being said about him, knew that she had been warned of his bad luck, and she had stood up in the face of her father's coldness, had said, "We are going for a ride." Flushed with it, with her defiance, and laughing at the way he remained stiff on the horse, remained so serious, while she rode beside him unafraid, utterly unafraid of anything. Coming to the lake, saying, "Let us stop here for a moment", because she wanted to be near him, wanted him to kiss her, was waiting for it, the ground spongy under their feet, watching the birds on the water, waiting for him to speak, to move, do something, but nothing, and she pointed at the ducks, said almost angrily in her frustration, "Why should the males have all the colours?" He had laughed then, laughed freely, his head back, taking her hand, saying, "You are my little drake", kissing her at last, and she had loved him.

But there was no riding now. No money for it at first, not for a long time, and later, when they were better off, James had bought the carriage horses and a fine hunter for himself. Nothing for her. It was not safe, as with everything in the colony, not safe for her to go anywhere, to do anything, to set foot outside the house. "Then why are we here?" she had said once. "Why are we here if it is so unsafe?" He had looked at her coldly, said that if she wished to ride she could go with him, she could ride one of the carriage horses, she need only ask. But whenever she asked, he had been busy, had said, "Not today, I have not the time. Perhaps we might go tomorrow, or next week."

At times she had wondered if she were being punished, for speaking out, for questioning him, for her family's disapproval, or some other, greater crime of which she was unaware. It felt that way often, that she had done something despicable, something so vile to make him hate her as he did. Punishing her, always punishing her. That time he had accepted an invitation from the governor's wife, for Caroline to accompany herself and her children to the menagerie at Green Point. She had wanted to decline, having grown nervous of company, but James had answered for her, saying how generous, how kind, she would be delighted, and for two nights she did not sleep, could not think what she might speak of, having read nothing, done nothing, been nowhere. Afraid of silence and afraid to fill it, afraid of disappointing James, who counted on good connections. "If you are going to be this way," he had said, "I won't allow you these excursions any longer, not if if you are to work yourself into such a state," making it seem like care, yet surely it was a threat, a threat of further punishment? And no way to avoid it, for how could she know what he wanted: angry if she went out, angry if she didn't, angry if she felt grief or fear, angry if she laughed, angry no matter what she said.

Nervous throughout the carriage ride, crushed in with the governor's wife, her large hat, her children and the slave girl. All of them noisy and jolly and singing, so that soon she had a headache and could not bear the thought that they had not even reached the menagerie yet, that the outing was still to be had, with who knows how many hours until she could be home again in silence. Yet once they were there, had room to breathe, the children running about, calling back from time to time, "Look, Mama, look at that!" and the governor's wife so calm and gentle, the headache had left her and she was able to walk amongst the cages, seeing the lion, the rhinoceros, the giraffe.

Then they were leaving, and there was a man outside with a hand-painted sign that read PONY RIDES. The pony had been garlanded and feathered, seemed exotic in its finery, even more so than the wild beasts. The children begged to be allowed to ride it, and Caroline had spoken out, afterwards hardly able to believe that she had done it, had said, "Oh, please do let them have a ride, allow me to pay, I would like to give them a little treat." Such excitement and squabbling over who would go first, being helped onto the old pony's back and being led round a worn track, sitting there like kings and queens, while she caught their excitement, held onto it, carrying it back home with her.

Wishing to have that moment again, taking weeks to ask James whether they might go, thinking he would refuse, as ever. He had sighed at the nuisance, another silly fancy of hers, but he had taken her the following Sunday, sullen all the way in the carriage, then holding her arm as they walked and looked at the dozing lion, a few ostriches, everything drab and wearisome. She could feel the resentment in the way he held her; this was what you wanted, wasn't it, this was what you asked for, so smile, enjoy it, be satisfied, for once be satisfied. Rushing to get through it all, wanting it done with that they might leave, that she could get away from this disappointment. Not even glancing in the direction of the pony when they left, because everything had been spoiled already, and what did it matter now, the garlands, the smiling children, the memories of laughter?

Her tongue thick upon waking; thick with fat from the meat of the blackfish, and thick, too, with sand that had blown across the beach all night. Though she had wrapped her head in the cloak, had covered her body in her torn skirt, it had come to her, sitting now within her mouth, upon her lips and between her fingers; all those places where the grease had cooled and set.

Stretching, then placing her hand on one of the giant bleached bones amongst which she had taken shelter, pushing herself up, rubbing her fingers together as she walked down to the water, trying to rid herself of the film of grease that made everything feel strange underhand. It began to crumble a little at the friction, to heat into slim cords of fat and sand that she flicked away from her, her lips working the same way, taking in the rolled peelings, spitting them out.

Strong wind off the water, waves crashing hard and white with froth near to the shore. Moving away from them, down towards a rock pool where the water was gentler, shivering quietly. The sea dark yet with night, soft at the edges with the colours that were to become the day. Raising her skirt, trying to tuck it up that it might stay dry, but the wind whipped hair into her face, and she lifted a hand to clear it from her eyes and mouth, letting the skirt tumble as she did. There was the weight of water at once, pulling her down, and she stepped back a little, afraid.

On the beach, a few continued to work on the carcass. What remained now was still useful to them, but the wind and exhaustion had driven many to curl up, as she had done, or else to take shelter in their small cottages on the low slopes on the other side of the wagon road. For a moment she let herself wonder what it might be like, a cottage of her own. To wake and sleep as she wished, to gather seashells for a garden path, to grow flowers and arrange them in jars on the windowsills, to sit in the sun morning or afternoon, greeting her neighbours, watching the passersby. But she could imagine none of it clearly, too caught within the pattern of her life, so that her wondering returned always to her duties, to the vegetable garden, the cycle of cooking and cleaning, the early mornings, the late nights. Even as she stood on the beach, watching the blackfish reduced to bones, it seemed as though she were elsewhere, that she had, in fact, never left the inn where she had lived all those years, that she had woken this day as on any other and gone to the barn to the warm udders of the cow, and that she would stay there, filling the same pail with milk, hour after hour, day after day, never able to leave.

Something foul rose up within her, and she heaved blackly onto the sand.

He moved now beyond the confines of his map, moving away from the lines and colours into a blank space, but even as he rode, the map was extending and he was building roads and bridges, creating villages and industries. He saw a solitary farmhouse with a gabled roof, a small forest of pine trees, a burnt-out cottage with an overturned wagon in the yard, a falcon sitting on the remains of a hind wheel, watching him, then taking off slowly as he passed. The sun rising swiftly, farmland glowing all around; dozens of wheat fields pale with stubble after the recent harvest; vines growing low and full. He was unsettled, this vastness, the long views, the waiting land. It ought to be put to some better use, it ought to be something more.

Stopping beside two labourers, calling them to a halt. They were going slowly, had hoes flung over their shoulders, one of them walking with a bandy-legged limp. He asked if they knew where Richard Percy's land was and they scanned the horizon, the waiting fields, as though the answer lay there, then shook their heads, said no, they knew only the farmers and none by that name. "Not a farm," said James, "just land," and the man with the limp pointed away from them, said, "There's wild land that way."

Pushing his horse on, crossing from the road into a field where a hottentot herder sat smoking a pipe as a flock of sheep and goats fed on the stubbled remains of the harvest. The ground uneven, soil soft, riding carefully, his eyes on what lay before, a gentle rise of land that kept the near distance from view. Coming to a stop at the summit, the field abruptly giving way to boulders and an overgrowth of scrub and trees.

FIRST OF DECEMBER

He dropped from his horse, tying its bridle to a branch, then pushed his way through dry bushes and long grass into the untouched land. The labourer had called it wild, and here it was, exactly that, a wilderness. Birds singing loudly in the trees and scrub, hopping amongst the leaves, chattering, diving, insects humming, and he pressed forward, breaking the twigs and branches that obstructed him, gloves smeared green with their sap. There was still the scent of fresh vegetables in his nostrils from the wagons before, but with this destruction that earthiness was replaced by something sharper, something more vibrantly alive. He reached forward, wanted to grab hold of it, that scent, that thing, imagining it altered, improved, the life of it even more vibrant, more dazzling, branches snapped off, trees uprooted, the land flattened, scrub cleared. Rocks could be levered out, the large ones blasted with gunpowder. No more than a fortnight for digging the foundations, six weeks, maybe eight, for basic construction. Easily done if he could get the lumber beforehand, be certain of a good supply of bricks. Possibly a hundred flats in the tenement, maybe more, as many as could be squeezed onto the land, and all of it done, ready, leased and making money by Easter.

He was counting on his fingers, murmuring numbers to himself, when a mongoose ran out from under a bush and stopped just ahead of him, sniffing the air, watching him with small black eyes. He moved slowly, reaching for the revolver he had brought with him, cocking it as quietly as he could, taking aim. But the animal was gone before he could fire, had run off into the mess of scrub and weeds. Still, he shot after it, birds scattering at the sound, leaves quivering where they had been, and "Two thousand" he said at the jolting of his hand. That had been the number in his mind when the animal appeared, the shot releasing it from him, pushing it out into the wilderness. He felt other words waiting to be spoken, other numbers and plans, and remained still as the leaves settled, the birds returned, then fired again, and again, taking aim at all these hindrances, the savagery of the land, letting his words tumble into it. A Cape robin fell with the last of the shots, the revolver hot in his right hand, swapping it to the left, moving through the scrub, keeping his head low, reaching the spot where the bird lay. Feeling the lightness of it in his palm, weighing nothing, yet as warm as the revolver. All around him the call of birds, the fresh morning leaves, and the glimmer of gun smoke.

FIRST OF DECEMBER

At first she ate nothing, uncertain whether he would return for breakfast and whether she ought to wait for him. Pouring a cup of tea after a while, picking at cubed pieces of melon. The tea bitter, having steeped too long, so she added sugar, but then did not drink it, simply sat looking at the gold pattern of the porcelain against the white background. A small chip on the rim, scratches in the gold, and she thought rather than felt that she should be upset about it, the set a wedding gift from her sister, meant for entertaining. James had brought out all their finest possessions since moving to the house on the Heerengracht, everything that had been stored away in chests, wrapped in straw and cloths, items they had not needed when living near the barracks. "This is the place for them, we must be seen to live well," he had said.

Raising her gaze now to the opposite wall, tilting her head, listening as though she might hear his footsteps outside above the sound of carts and hooves and morning cries. Watching four squares of light from the window stretch and shudder on the wall, spreading across to the dark frame of a watercolour she had painted herself, showing the mountain, parts of the town. Done in the early days, finding ways to occupy herself, painting scenes of Cape life to send home, hoping someone would see something in them and say how charming, how lovely, what a paradise, how fortunate you are! But they saw only what was barbarous, foreign, strange, and she knew it was she herself who had painted that into the pictures. A fire in this one, taking over the mountain, as they often did, said to be started from the camps of runaway slaves, gangs of them roaming the lower reaches of the mountain, robbing passersby. Fires often returning to her, coming to her in dreams, in quiet moments, flames at her back, moving in on all sides, destroying the town, working its way through the streets and avenues, trees and buildings shivering into ash, the whole of the land on fire, and no choice but to flee to the shore, board a ship, go home.

Morning light crept across the frame, the fire in the sun-faded picture coming to life again, everything ablaze, everything hot and flaming. "Let it burn," she thought, "let it burn," so real the heat, the smell that she was ready to rise, to run, and she did rise, going to the window, moving aside the lace to look out at the mountain. But it was green and grey as ever, the sky still and blue.

Returning to the table, sitting with her back to the window and the watercolour, staring into her lap, removing her rings, trying them on different fingers, none feeling right, and she could not think of wearing them, felt them to be garish, heavy. Taking them with the tips of her fingers, reaching across the table to put them on the saucer beside the chipped cup. No place set in front of her, and she picked up the plate from James's seat at the head of the table, smoothed the tablecloth, put the plate down. Not wanting anything, yet, looking for bread, meaning to take a slice, make a pretence of having eaten. But the loaf was still wrapped in its cloth and she had to uncover it, feeling the steaming warmth in her palm, the fresh release of heat as she cut into it. Wanting it now, wanting all of it, but not to eat, not for eating. Cutting again, a larger slice, and another, even larger, full and warm, pressing her fingers into the soft, moist texture, seeing the marks of the knife, the dents left by her fingertips. Standing up, pressing down with force, sawing the knife back and forward, the loaf flattening under the weight of her hand. Reaching now for an apple from the fruit bowl, cutting that in halves and then quarters, doing the same to a quince, a pear. Lifting a strawberry from a jar of preserve, holding it down with two fingers, carving into it with the knife, cutting it first into slivers, and then across, into tiny squares. Moving around the table to the vulgarity of a cured ham, pink and large, the knife red with syrup and fruit, marking the meat with it as she cut, making it appear grazed and bleeding. This was it: a knife in her heart, at her throat, her stomach, her wrists. This was everything being and going.

Leah came in, saw the mess on the table, the fruit, the mangled loaf and ham, said, "Oh, miss," and took the knife away from her.

She sat down, began to cry. The watercolour again, the sunlight on the wall, the memory of fire, of blood. Leah's hand on hers, "Please, miss, don't cry. Let's try not to cry today." Gripping the girl's hand, this hand, this hand, the only one that ever came near her. This rough hand that dressed her, combed her hair, cleaned her and fed her, cared for every part of her. Lifting it to her face, pressing it against her cheek, looking up at her, her dark freckles, her mud-coloured eyes.

The girl smiled, brought her other hand to Caroline's face, held her like that, then touched her cheek to Caroline's forehead, rested it there, feeling for a temperature. "Are you not well, miss? Would you like to lie down?"

That touch, that hand on her, reminding her of the first

days after her sickness, when she had been still weak, hardly able to move by herself, having to wait for Leah to help her from the bed, her arm around her waist, walking slowly across the room to a chair beside the window, sitting there while Leah changed the sheets, sprinkled the bed with lavender water, the smell of sickness strongest in the mornings. The same smell on her nightgown, and on her skin, where still there were sores that wept. Leah helped her off with the nightgown, lifting her a little so that she could pull it out from beneath her, then washed her, the sores stinging, no matter how gently she touched them. Having to stand after that, holding onto the arm of the chair while Leah washed between her legs, saying, "Only a moment longer, miss, almost done." Then on with a clean nightgown, and sitting once more to have a comb pulled through those hairs that had not fallen out. Finally, the slow walk to bed, a sip of sweet tea, already gone cold, before lying back on the pillows and falling into shadowed sleep.

Waking early one morning, calling for Leah, wanting something, some food or drink, a fierce craving for salt and sweet, a mix of the two, for jam and meat, or sugar in beef tea. But Leah did not come, and she tried getting up by herself, tired of the bed, the exhausting confinement. Movement slow, but she had her feet on the ground, was able to push herself up after a few attempts, holding herself steady on the frame of the bed, standing there with trembling legs. Calling for Leah again, but catching sight of herself in the mirror across the room, staring for a moment at the hideous stranger she had become. Sitting back down in fright, afraid of how much she had altered. Realising that she had not seen her face in months, that Leah had kept mirrors from her, and she wondered how else she had changed, what other ghastliness was on her. Pushing herself up once more, walked unsteadily to the corner of the bed, holding onto the post for support, turning so that she could see the mirror properly, and withdrawing her nightgown. Her breasts limp and sagging with the weight she had lost, ribs sharp, hips jutting out, her body marred by sores and bruises, rashes still fading. But even there, beyond these markers of decay, there seemed to be a quickening, a call to life. Touching her collar bones, her loose thighs, stroked her balding pubis, remembering what she had been to James at one time, dropping down onto the bed, sitting first on the edge, then lying back, giving in to the ecstasy of touch, feeling the sheets beneath her naked skin, feeling herself as she wished James to feel her. As clear and direct as if it were happening, his hands on her, being loved, being kissed and wanted and admired. The feel of her body, the increase of warmth and passion, until her neck arched, her mouth flew open.

Leah finding her like that, saying, "Come, miss, this won't do," dressing her again and placing her under the covers, pulling the sheets up to her chin, her hand on her forehead, "Sleep now, miss, go to sleep."

There was the blur of Table Mountain in the distance, the white clouds above it. Pushing the horse towards them, back to the town and noise, angry now, furious, galloping past vineyards, grazing flocks, angry, angry, because he must have that land, he must have it. Feeling still the warmth of the dead robin in his hand, the soft feathers, the blood, a speck of something, some insect or berry on its beak, and being surprised by that, that sign that it had been alive, had been living, a brief moment of wonder at this small thing, and then the fury, sudden and vile, rising up through him. Crushing the bird in his fist, feeling the bowing of the feathers, the cracking of tiny bones, and a dart of shit squirting out onto his glove. Throwing the bird down in disgust, standing up from where he had been crouching, his thighs burning at the sudden movement, trying to wipe the shit from him with a leaf, but making it worse, a long smudge across his palm. Riding back home with his anger like a stain all over him, because he had known before speaking to Percy that he did not have the capital to buy the land.

But he could not be blamed for his debts, it was not his fault, all of them were essential. That was what had never been understood, his family washing their hands of him, even now, after all his successes, everything achieved through his own insight, his own determination, they never understood what had to be done in order to make any sort of headway, that commerce was built on credit. Hugo long since refusing to have anything to do with him, calling him a swindler and gambler to anyone who would listen. Leonard no better, making it clear that the inheritance he had received when his father died was to be the last, there was to be no more. He thought of borrowing from one of the Dutch widows, as he had done previously in times of need, but they could not be relied upon to be discreet. How would it look if it became known that, on the eve of opening a new bank, he found it necessary to take out a large loan?

He had reached the town once more, the streets busy with carts and labourers, slave apprentices carrying bundles of wood, errand boys running to and fro, maidservants sweeping doorsteps, and drunks being kicked up from where they lay, leaving them staggering through the streets, looking for a place to set themselves down again. Everything busy and moving, and he had no patience for delays, rushing past them, knocking a woman over in his haste, a basket of cabbages tumbling into the street, but he did not stop, only looked down to curse her, her cabbages, her slow, gossiping stride, and drove his horse on. Wanting to get somewhere, he must get somewhere, arrive at a plan, some solution, not the widow, not family. Finding as he moved through alleys and side streets that he was making his way towards the Exchange, the stifling rooms, the brass and mahogany sign, and that was it, that was the answer! There was money, plenty of it, money that he could take with ease, using it first to buy the land, start construction, maybe even pay off some his debts. Yes, all of that was possible, borrow it briefly, hardly for any length of time, just a matter of days, or perhaps weeks, then return it, and the investors need never know.

Coming to a halt, his thoughts cut short at the sudden stop, caught behind a queue of wagons and carts, waiting as a funeral procession passed up towards the Heerengracht and the Dutch church. More than twenty hired mourners, dressed in various shades of black, walking sombrely after the hearse which had been raised to an ostentatious height by the addition of black plumes. Watching idly, trying to return to his plan, pick it up where he had dropped it, yes, the money, the bank, the land and his debts, yet there remained still the problem of how to pay it back, of where to find the money in so short a time. The auction of goods salvaged from the Dunlop would bring in no more than a pittance.

Sitting astride his horse, watching with impatience, drumming his fingers on his thigh, if only they would hurry up, move faster. Did the whole town have to come to a standstill just because someone had died? But then, even as he adjusted himself in the saddle, his anger turned to grief, remembering coming back from London after his most recent visit, landing still with his sea legs and laughing about them as he stumbled across the dirty shore. Stone waiting for him, telling him of Caroline's illness, and he had not waited for a carriage, had run all the way up the Heerengracht to their home, arriving out of breath, finding her half dead, barely recognisable. Always that fear with him now, that little knot that had made him throw himself on her lap, press his face into her stomach and say, "Do not leave me."

Watching the procession, and it was certain, yes, it was she who had died, he had arrived too late, had not made it to the house, was still running up from the shore on his sea legs, and there she was, that was her passing in the hearse, her for whom the mourners were keening. But there were not enough of them, there had to be more, fifty at least, a hundred, the whole town, in fact, everybody should be grieving, and he must arrange a tombstone, a large one, engraved with the words "Here lies CAROLINE beloved wife of JAMES KENDRICK, founder of the First Colonial Bank, philanthropist and businessman", then some embellishment, some angel, or bouquet of calla lilies, something decorative and fine. What would Hugo say of that, he wondered, there could be no criticism of that, no shame, not of that finery, better even than the family vault at home. Let Hugo come, let Leonard, and anyone else who had doubted him, let them come and see for themselves what he was in the eyes of the city. No longer that man they had thought him, that embarrassment who had returned at last from America, having managed to earn enough to travel third class, and arriving thin, lice-infested, scabbed and weak, with not a penny, walking to Lord Ingelsby's house and being taken in. Later there was no welcome from his father, only reprimands for not having used the servant's entrance when in that state, for allowing himself to be seen in the streets, for not using an alias, and what would Lord Ingelsby's neighbours have thought, was that the way to treat an old family friend?

But suddenly it was all gone, he was sinking, sinking, and there was no bank, no properties, it was him alone suddenly, alone in his poverty, with his failures, and the shame of giving Caroline a pauper's burial, with an unmarked grave, the humiliation, that dreadful humiliation of what they would say, the people of the town, of how he would appear to them. He must sell something. Anything. He must find something to sell, make money somehow, thinking of her jewellery, several expensive rings, a number of necklaces, one of opal and diamonds, another with emeralds, and there were more, heirlooms and gifts that he knew of. Already in his mind ransacking her dressing table, going through her drawers and trinket boxes. Finding them there, at the back of one of the drawers, what he had forgotten she had: her shares, left to her when her father died three years before. Her father having written to him in the preceding months, a long letter in a trembling hand, accusing James of having lied and cheated, of betraying them all, and how he worried for his Caroline, who had been better to James than he had ever deserved. "We both know the law," the old man had written, "we understand that women may not inherit, but I want to believe this one final time, for my own sake and for Caroline's, that you will be honourable, that you may be trusted. I will say nothing of what you have done already. That cannot be undone. I ask now that you do not touch the shares I shall leave to her. Let me die with that peace of mind, I beg you." James had once again promised that he could be trusted, speaking of all his businesses, his plans, saying there was no need for using her inheritance, not with his achievements as they were.

Yet here he was, and he needed money, and there she was in that hearse. The dead needed no promises.

The horse snorted, stamped its hoof. James saw that the procession had passed, that the waiting wagons and carriages were moving forward. He knew, of course he knew, that Caroline was not dead, that that was not her corpse going up towards the church. Yet, it was true, wasn't it, absolutely true that she might well have died, that she might in fact still die, after all she was unwell, could die at any moment. What difference was there in using the shares to pay for her funeral or for buying land? And after all, the law viewed the shares as his, they were legally his, whether she were alive or dead. No one could dispute that. It would not be wrong; he would be doing nothing wrong.

Writing to Percy when he reached home, enclosing the shares, explaining that they were worth more than the asking price for the land, but he would sign all of them over if Percy would accept them as payment immediately. Coming out of his study into the passage, feeling himself a lord, a king, a god, straddling the mountain, the town, the lands beyond, everything spreading out beneath his shadow. But then he paused, dropped his hands to his side. Caroline stood at the bottom of the stairs, watching him, her face pale, white, having returned from the death he had wished upon her.

By late morning the wind had settled and there was only heat, baking the rocks and scrub around her. She was ill, her ascent slow, and several times had to stop to relieve herself of the fat and meat that churned inside her. Each time she thought the worst was over, but the cramps continued. Leaning over rocks, tasting salt and fat, weighed down with the fever of them, wanting to lie down, wanting nothing more than to lie down somewhere cool. Looking for shade, considering even the small patches under bushes that scratched at her with their thorns and sharp leaves, but she kept going forward, driven by a need for water.

At times she found herself at the inn, changing sheets on the beds, washing them, hanging them, beating them, scrubbing floors, serving food. There were men in her face, voices loud with liquor, saying things to her, demanding things of her, and then she would come to with a start, find herself alone on the mountain once more, unable to tell what was dream or wish or memory. Fever and cramps inhabiting everything, and she was ill in all places and times, throughout the past, in this moment, and far into the future.

Hearing someone say her name, believing it to be September, believing him to have been living on the mountain all this time, waiting for her. She stumbled, turned, calling to him, "Hold on, I'm coming, I'm coming," and she was giving birth again, the cramps, the nausea and pain, but this time he would be with her, this time their little girl would live, if only she could reach him. "I'm here, I'm coming, I'm here, wait for me," then finding him at last, seeing him seated in the shade, his back against an outjutting of rock, legs stretched out before him. The baby moving within her at the sight of him, coming to them, to be with them.

The smell of shit roused her, made her pause, standing still for a while, watching him where he sat, his face obscured by a hat she did not recognise. Flies moved around him, buzzed in and out of the hat's shade. He seemed to be asleep, and she whispered his name, waited, then whispered it again. He did not look up. The smell kept her back, made her afraid of approaching. She picked up a pebble, threw it to the side, away from them both. He made no move at the sound, seemed not to have heard it, the flies continuing at his face. She waited a while longer, the baby coming, ready to come, almost there, and she was desperate with fever, desperate for water, for his arms around her, to be with him again. Moving forward, "Please, wake up, I'm here, we're here, please, we've come." Still he did not move, but she could see him more clearly now, could see by his skin colour as he began to separate out from the shade and rock that it could not be September, that this man was too dark, Mozambican perhaps, and old, far too old. She knew then, at once understood the smell and the flies, that he was dead, that he had soiled himself in dying.

She could not tell in all this wilderness where he might have been going. He seemed to have been living here for a few days at least, by the looks of the fire, and the way his possessions had been placed around him. Afraid at first, remembering the stories of the dead, their horrible possession of the living, but the cramps were strong, and she began to feel something coming out of her, leaking down the backs of her legs. It was her baby, she knew, her little girl born dead once more. "You see, I am here, we came", she said to the old man, going over to where he sat, feeling no fear now, not when she had already been possessed by death in this way, carrying inside her a sharp repetition of loss, endless loss.

Lying down beside him, asking if she might have some of his water, taking a gourd from his stiffened hand, drinking it down in one go. The cramps intensifying at first, gripping her stomach, feeling there the crying grief of her little girl, her small, infant rage. Falling asleep in that clenching pain, and twice startled awake by dreams in which she found the man staring at her with great eyes, dark as the eyes of the blackfish. In another he took hold of her arm, pulled her towards him.

At the last she sat up. Hours had passed and night had fallen. Her cramps were gone. Reaching her hand across to where he sat, feeling rather than seeing his open eyes, letting her fingertips close them, saying a prayer she had been taught as a child, the words seeming worth very little. Then looking through his possessions, finding a small bag of coffee grounds, a bit of sugar, a pouch of cheap tobacco, and a piece of paper on which something was written. She could not read, yet it seemed important, so she placed it beside him, anchored by a stone, thinking that perhaps it was his name, or that of someone he loved. Wondering what else she might do or say before leaving, but already it felt as though he had faded into the rocks, was part of this mountain and wilderness, and she wondered if this too would be her fate – to die alone amongst the rocks and live in that grey eternity.

FIRST OF DECEMBER

All evening seeing its gaunt face across the table from him, watching its dry lips, its brittle hair. Torture to have it right in front of him, this living corpse, its bony hands bringing food to its mouth, then clutching at a glass of wine, sputtering at the first sip, having to put the glass down with a clatter amongst the knives. Its chest heaving, the collar bones sharpening as it leaned forward, pulling at the tablecloth in an attempt to rise, coughing still, looking at him with alarm. But he could do nothing, watched the red spittle land on the tablecloth, the face turn dark. In his mind he was patting her on the back, pouring a glass of water for her, holding it to her lips, but he could not bring himself to get up, could not find the will to approach this thing, to touch her in her death. She coughed with greater force, was trying to push herself up, moving along the table towards him. A drop of spittle flew onto his cheek, felt hot as a curse.

Leah came in, rushing to put aside the dish of strawberries she was carrying, taking Caroline's arm, stroking her back, giving it one hard slap, forcing her to stand up straight, before making her swallow more of the wine. It went down this time, Caroline gasping afterwards, then hiccupping, clutching her chest, hiccupping again. She sat down, drank more with trembling hands, and he cleared his throat, asked if she was all right. Yes, she said, yes, just a cough, nothing really, but would he mind if she went to bed? He was still holding his knife and fork, noticed them only now, his dinner half-eaten. He could not look at her, looked instead at the plate, moved the food around with his fork while he replied that of course she may go, she must not exhaust herself on his account. Leah helped her up, led her from the room, and he saw the little curls at the back of Caroline's head, growing from the pink memory of the bedsore that had been there.

Afterwards he tried to right the tablecloth, the dishes and cutlery clanking as he moved it, Caroline's glass falling over, wine spilling, and he built a dam around it with his serviette to prevent it dripping onto the floor, seeing it pool thickly and soak into the fabric. Getting up, going into the parlour, feeling in his pocket for a cigar, finding none, looking on the mantlepiece, a side table, kicking at the animal skins on the floor, feeling the hideous discomfort of guilt, her pale face, her pale dead face, killing her over and over in his mind, watching her die in her bed, watching her die at the table.

Then lay down on the couch, bringing an imaginary cigar to his lips. Her face, her face, firm within him, that dreadful, dying face. Picking up an embroidered cushion, made during one of her fads some years before, but always she lost interest, could never enjoy anything for long, miserable, miserable, always so miserable. Covering his eyes with it, but even then the image remained in his mind, and he felt again the spittle on his cheek, saw her fierce bone edges. He needed brandy, was about to ring for Leah, but it was he who kept the key to the liquor cabinet, he who must unlock it, pour for himself, lock it again. Sitting up, putting his hand down on the seat of the couch. Caroline had left one of her women's magazines there, he could feel it beneath him as he shifted, lifting it up, holding it before him. She had left it open to a page where there was a colour engraving of a woman, the caption reading "London evening wear". He had only picked it up to move it out of the way, was about to close it, but found that he could not, the woman surprisingly familiar, her expression, the tilt of her neck. This was Caroline he was looking at, an earlier version of her, that hair, the extravagant costume, the beauty that was hard to remember when he saw her these days, so fragile, skeletal. In this page she was returned to him, and he was with her, was dancing with her, remembering the froth and frills of balls, the laughter, the twirling warmth. Remembering, too, standing with her beside a lake, how she had said she would never be drab, and "drake" he had called her, holding her, feeling her waist, her lips, the taste of her, and she had been everything then, all colours, all beauty. He wanted that again, wanted that laughter, that colour, that love.

Thursday
29th November 1838

The dress stayed with him, shook him into unrest, lifting him out of himself, setting him down in a ballroom, into memories and dreams, had him spinning, spinning, all night on his feet, waking up with the bedclothes bunched in his arms, shaped to a woman's body, feeling the excitement of it between his legs, against his chest, his cheek. He knew what he would do, going into the parlour, finding the magazine where he had left it on the couch. He had closed it the night before, had to flip through it now to find the engraving, missing it the first time, going too fast, having to page through it again, slowly, licking his forefinger, turning page by page. Then, when he had found it, taking hold of the top corner, pulling too eagerly, the paper coming out jagged, half the skirt left behind. He thought of tearing it out too, perhaps pasting the two parts together, but there was no time for that, no time, and he had enough of the picture in his hand, enough for the vision to be clear.

Going to the seamstress Caroline used, banging on the door until she opened it, flustered, still with her wrapper on, her hair in disarray under her day cap, but smiling when she saw who it was, inviting him in. No, he would not stop for tea, he was in haste, showing her the page from the magazine, saying it had to be done by the next afternoon, that everything else must be put aside, he would pay what was necessary, money was no object, but could she do it, was it possible? She took hold of the engraving, looked it over, nodding, it was possible, yes, but not easy, and certainly not cheap. She would put all her girls to work on it at once, with so many hands it would be complete in time, she had no doubt about that, he need have no fear, and may she say how wonderful, what a generous husband he was, there were not many as good as he in this part of the world.

He came out into the street, still with the dress in his mind, the scent of fresh flowers, a balcony on a cool star-filled night, taking off a glove to touch her neck with the tip of his finger, tracing it along her jawline, the soft ridges of her shoulders and collar bones, then kissing her beneath each earlobe, feeling her breath on him, whispering something, he could not remember what, something tender, kissing her mouth, with her hands at the back of his head as he pressed her into the railing while others danced no more than a few feet away in the ballroom. Afterwards she had hummed a part of a tune; a thing she had often done in moments of happiness or thought, a sound that never failed to make him sit up, look across at her with desire. Wishing to hear it now, anything, any song, to dance, to sing, have that feeling of rushing in from the balcony into the ballroom, moving together, her dress all around him, the sound of those notes in his head, vibrating through him.

Nearby a beggar sat in a doorway, scratching at fleabites on her exposed legs. She reached out when she saw James, said, "Please, master, please, I need to eat." She was old, had a few white hairs on her chin, wore nothing but a threadbare dress, a ragged shawl. The top of her chest was exposed, showed black scars, a brand mark that had erupted and grown. Again the woman said, "Please, master, some food."

He stopped a moment, tossed a coin to her, continued with his humming. She scrabbled for it now between her folded legs, James watching idly, the tune growing into an agitation. "Do you sing?" he said. "I want a song, I'm looking for a song." He had more coins in his fist, shook them at the woman.

"A song?"

"This one, do you know it?" He sang, giving it nonsense words. "La-la-la ta-loo too-too."

The woman shook her head, said she only knew one song, had forgotten most of the words by now.

"Go on, let's have it anyhow, let's try," said James.

The woman began uncertainly, her voice croaking, off-key. "Al is er ons prinsje nog zo klein—"

But James stopped her. "No, no, you can't sing like that. On your feet, get up, stand up." He moved his arms, his legs. "We dance, like this, come on, we dance."

The woman struggled up, holding on to the wall. Her legs were weak, thin as bones. She sang the first verse, stopped, said she knew no more.

"No, no, it's this I want, try this." James sang the tune again, cocking his head as the woman tried to echo him. "That's it, but louder, louder, it has to be louder. Now the dance, like this, a twirl now, that's right, and again," conducting with his cane, moving up and down in front of her, filled with his urgency, while the old woman shuffled desperately, trying to sing louder and louder, until James noticed damp spreading beneath her on the dusty road, realising then that she had wet herself with the effort.

FIRST OF DECEMBER

Dirt under a fingernail, and no idea from where it might have come. She had washed her face and hands before bed, had been nowhere since, not wanting to get up this morning, saying she felt weak, unwell. She wanted to lie in, did not want breakfast. Yet Leah had brought a cup of tea and a dry biscuit she said was commonly eaten amongst the Dutch, that it would be good for her, that it was fed to the ill and old, but it was too hard, too thick to bite into, and she left it on the saucer.

Lying back, willing herself to be unwell, feeling the weakness coming up through her, there it was, sitting in her bones, in her head, all of her weak and halting, impossible to get up, to move, to speak. Wishing for it, for more of it, this pain, this heaviness of limb, wishing to be bedbound again, to return to that dark tunnel of her illness. Yet at the same time tired of it already, tired of this bed, this room, her own wearying thoughts, rolling over, crying without tears, her breath harsh with sleep, with the tea, always Leah made it too sweet, always this offense against her, every morning, her gums burning with the sweetness. Wanting water, to rinse out her mouth, but unable to move, to call.

Then Leah was beside her again, pulling the sheets back and, "Oh don't," she said, pushing her face into the pillow, "don't", Leah laughing, saying, "Come on, come on, up you get." But "Don't!" she said again, angry, and Leah stood with the sheets in her arms, her smile going, waiting a moment, looking to the window where the curtains were still drawn, saying they might go for a walk before too long, only she had some chores to do, had to get the washing to the laundrywoman who was waiting outside. And Caroline pushed herself up from the pillow, weak, weak, how to get up with this dreadful weight, this weight of her limbs, this weight of living? But even as she stood the illness was going from her, even as she said "Help me" she knew she needed no help, and she was angry at it, at her lie, shouting at Leah to get out, get out, leaning against the dressing table, feeling strong enough to push it over.

The heat of the afternoon upon her, lying like sickness along the lower slopes of the mountain and extending out into the veld, the earth black and grey, with stumps turned to coal. In places the shells of tortoises, skeletons of snakes or lizards. Beyond that, only a monotony of ash. Nothing moving amongst the grey, everything dragging towards death, and she herself part of that exertion.

Yet her nausea had passed, the diarrhoea and cramps gone, most of her wounds dried and crusted over, itchy on her face and legs, only a circle still pulsating hotly on her forearm, made worse by the sun beating down on it. The scab had never fully dried, remained yellow and raised. Lifting it with her fingernails, peeling it back easily at first, watching the release of pus, but it caught in one section, held fast by the skin around it, and she had to pull harder, feeling the rip, the sting, seeing the blood where it had been attached, putting her mouth there, to the heat, to the metallic raw taste of herself, as though all of her skin had been removed, her entire body exposed, every bit of her flesh, everything tender within her. Throughout the day flies continued to come to that single spot, sitting on it, tasting it. Drawn back to it herself, to the taste of pain, her tongue working it, taking nervous comfort in its presence.

The midday horizon held the heat, was in motion with it, an uneven glowing haze, everything dull and muddled. But as she went on, she began to see growths coming out of the ash and coal, leaves unfurling, shockingly green against the grey. With every step coming upon more, unable to avoid treading on them, their springing softness beneath her soles.

All the dullness, all the death altered now, the whole of that bleak landscape touched by abundance. A heady scent, of vibrant life, of every stone, every flower and petal, of the hot sand. She had known there was life in the wilderness, knew it from the early mornings, the dark nights she had come from, the sounds of insects and frogs, of creatures calling to one another, saying, as she had done to September, "I am here, I am here".

Now, in this havering stillness, this shimmering heat, seeing a cottage in the distance, hearing a donkey's mournful braying. Drawing nearer, watching a woman, servant or slave, come out into the yard, empty a pail, go back inside quickly, ducks and geese, a few chickens, all rushing noisily towards the scraps. Then two slave apprentice boys came from around the corner of the house, carrying firewood, kicking out at the fowl, trying to clear a path through them. One of the geese straightened its neck, spread its wings and hissed at them, while around it the others honked and quacked and clucked. The shorter of the boys drew back, but the taller rushed at it, chasing it off, wood falling from his arms as he did, then went on to the woodpile beside the back door and dropped his burden, the shorter boy following behind and doing the same. Both turned back and picked up the wood that had fallen, the shorter kicking at his half-heartedly, trying to move the pieces into place, the other bending down, packing his neatly.

After a while, the shorter picked up a piece of wood, threw it at the fowl that had returned to peck at scraps, waited for them to scatter, then walked a few steps towards where a water butt stood. He dipped his hands in it, splashed his face, dipped again, and drank from his hand before lowering the top of his head into the water, coming up, shaking drops from him. The taller turned and said something to him, she could not hear what. The shorter splashed his face again, more vigorously this time, then drew both hands up and smacked them palm-down on the water, directing the splash towards the taller boy. He jumped up at being wet, rushed across, shouting, and pushed the shorter in the chest. He fell back, but reached out and grabbed hold of the taller's shirt, pulling himself up. They were grappling now, arms around one another, falling, holding, pushing, rolling in the dust of the yard, and bumping hard into the water butt, hard enough that it tottered, water splashing out, soaking them.

The woman came outside, carrying a broom, began hitting them with the soft end. They let go of one another and moved apart, their legs and clothes muddied and torn. She scolded them, hit out a few more times, then made them stand up, pointing away from her, back in the direction from which the boys had come, and they walked towards it, their heads down as she continued to scold. When they had gone, she stood and shook her head at the spilled water, the messy yard, the scattered fowl, went to the water butt, peered in, shaking her head again, returning inside.

Having watched all this, having stood in silence and seen it all, she felt that she had been upon the mountain, had been living this fugitive life as long as she knew, that the inn, which before had seemed to sit inside her and refuse to leave, had somehow been removed from her, a hand reaching into her, grabbing it, ripping it out. But this world below, this world of geese and pails, of water and emotion, was alien and terrifying. Not knowing how to enter it, unable to think of words with which to go down to that woman and try to communicate, knowing only the wilderness's call of "I'm here, I'm here". Trying that, her voice a croak, a howl, waiting for a response, waiting to see whether the woman would come out of the cottage again, or perhaps the donkey might bray. But there was nothing, and she was alone in the shimmering heat.

FIRST OF DECEMBER

In the parlour, being brought more tea, another of the biscuits, being told, "It isn't so hard if you put it in the tea first. Really, it's very good, miss, try it. It is fortifying, they say." Waiting until Leah had left, picking up the biscuit and dipping it into the tea, holding it there for a while, lifting it out to find it had softened too much, the wet part separating from the rest, falling into the cup. She dropped what remained, the whole thing unappetising, a mess, and it splashed a little as it fell, droplets landing on the saucer, a few on her hand; noticing the dirt under her fingernail again, and walking across to the bureau where she wrote her correspondence, looking amongst the mess of paper and inkwells for a letter opener. She could find none, taking up a loose steel nib instead, curving it under the nail, lifting the dirt out, holding it up to her nose, unable to make out what it was, no smell to it, though it held the ochre colour of dust and dirt, and of everything around her.

The front door opened, the sound of his quick footsteps. She flicked the dirt away from her, suddenly ashamed of it, to be found with it, listening to the surprise of his heavy breathing, as though he had been running, and the same quick footsteps were going to the breakfast room, opening the door, rushing off again, up the stairs, walking along the passage, tapping at her bedroom door, opening it, saying her name, then back down the stairs, coming at last to the parlour, peering in, not seeing her at first, then noticing her standing beside the writing bureau and saying with a laugh, "Oh, there you are." A bundle of papers under his arm, holding them up. "Look, I've been to the Port Office. A ship came in yesterday, did you hear?", and she was irritated by this, where did he suppose she would have heard it from, who would have told her? "The James McInroy, or John McInroy, or something. See what it has brought for you."

She had left the bureau open, and he turned to it now, placing the bundle on it, going through the newspapers and letters he had fetched. "Here," he said, holding out a magazine, turning it slightly so that she could see the title. "Lady's Pocket Magazine. Only a few weeks out of date."

Taking it from him, saying thank you, trying to understand this strange enthusiasm, this breathlessness. He was smiling at her, watching as she walked over to the couch with the magazine. Not knowing what he wanted, picking up the small hand bell on the side table, ringing for Leah.

He put his hand on the open bureau, fiddled with a piece of loose paper, said, "You like your magazines, don't you?" smiling again, looking at her expectantly. "These fashions and such things, you have always liked them, haven't you?"

"I suppose so." Afraid that it was a trick, turning from him, opening the magazine, scanning the table of contents: the Language of Gloveology, Burchands Requirements for a Wife, Ancient Marriage Anecdotes, then finding the page for a serial she had been following, though when she glanced at the first paragraphs she could recognise none of the names nor the plot. For a moment she wondered whether she ought to look for the previous issue, read it again, but knew that she wouldn't, simply paging on now as James watched her, stopping briefly at an engravings of a castle in Baghdad, of a fairy in a garden of flowers.

"Yes," James said. "I remember."

Looking up, wanting to ask him what he was saying, what was it that he remembered, but Leah was entering with a tray, had brought a cup of tea for him. "No, not this. I want coffee, coffee," he said, gesturing with a wild hand towards the kitchen, though he took the cup and drank from it, holding it around the rim with three fingers, the handle turned away from him, gulping the contents down and then smacking his lips together. Sitting in a ladderback chair, leaning back, his hands on his thighs, standing again. "Whatever happened to that dress of yours?" he said.

"Which dress?" Again she was confused, suspicious, expecting to be trapped somehow, caught out.

"White, with, what would you call them – flounces – of pink all around the skirt, and a little something here." He fiddled at his shoulder.

"That was years ago."

"And your cousin, that awful one, Maria—"

"Margaret."

"Margaret, she tripped and spilled her glass of wine all down the front."

"It was punch, I think."

"Yes, punch. I never saw you wear it again."

"The stain wouldn't come out, no matter what Betsy tried. It has most likely long since been used up for rags."

Leah came in with a cup of coffee and he said, "Ah yes, exactly what I need, exactly this, thank you." Drinking it down as he had done with the tea, then moving about the room, saying, "What a morning I've had. Yes, quite a morning," coming to a standstill, putting his hands behind his back, raising himself up on his heels, then down again, doing that a few times, before walking across to the harp, plucking at its strings. The smile went, he looked at her, back at the harp. Here it was, here it was coming, and she steadied herself for it, the trap at last: a reproach for never having learnt to play, though he had bought her all the music and books she needed, had even arranged lessons, the teacher coming only once before his wife died in childbirth and he took the next ship home. James opened his mouth, and she was ready for it.

"I have been out this morning," he said at last, his hand still on the harp.

Waiting for more – What was this? What was this trick? – waiting, and when he did not continue, urging him on, pushing him towards this thing she wasn't understanding. "At the Port Office, you mean?"

He looked at her, frowned. "What? Oh, yes. I went there. And elsewhere too. I was in Buitenkant Street and...," fiddling with the handle of the coffee cup, picking it up again, drinking the last of it, then, "What news from Cassandra?"

She shook her head. "It is above three months since last I heard from her."

"Oh, yes, I forgot," he said, fumbling in his pocket, bringing out a letter, handing it across. "It came too, I forgot, with the magazine." And he seemed to drop, to fade, as she took it from him, the restlessness, the smiles, his strange enthusiasm utterly gone. He said no more, took the papers from the bureau, left the room.

The heat growing steadily fiercer, everything bristling with haze. Sand underfoot, burnt-out twigs catching at her skin, new, fresh growths wilting in the remorseless silence. Then something faint, something uncertain, a movement, a whispering, and she walked towards that sound, the blur of the heat making a red and black mirage. A bush on fire, a bush alive. But the blur evened out and she could see now that there were locusts, a hundred of them, casting off their outer shells and emerging fragile into the day.

Walking slowly towards the avenue, having to take Leah's arm for support, the morning's weakness back, anticipating the contents of Cassandra's letter, all the teas and luncheons and dinners, plays and operas and exhibitions, all that busyness with which she filled her life. Beginning to plan her reply, writing it in her mind, but finding, as always, that she had nothing to say. There had been the wreck of the Dunlop, the Infant School concert, the coming emancipation, the wind and dust. Nothing that would be of interest to her sister. She might mention the menagerie again, had written of it often before, making it seem as though they went there regularly, that it was ever expanding with exotic creatures that were a wonder to behold, keeping that phrase in her mind, "oh, so many wonders to behold, my dear Cassie, you would not believe the things I have seen, such animals, such birds," reminded then of one she had come across, not at the menagerie, it was elsewhere, and not alive. "What was that bird we saw?" she said to Leah. "The one that was stuffed and mounted, do you remember, with the blue and black feathers? Was it at Reid's Curiosity Shop, was that it?"

"Yes, miss."

"But where did it come from? Was it Guinea, is that what Mr Reid told us?"

"Yes, miss." Then pointing at a bench in the avenue, oak trees on either side, saying, "Here we are, miss, will you rest here a moment?"

Nodding, letting herself be helped in sitting down, Leah making her comfortable before stepping away from the bench, standing watch behind, close enough that she might be called if needed. People walking past, the day pleasant, the wind having died down at last, everyone taking advantage of the fine weather, though it was hot, approaching the middle of the day, and she knew that soon the heat would drive her indoors, but for now watching the people, the glow of the spring leaves, then finally removing the letter from her purse. It was a little crumpled, had a smudge at the address, her name half obliterated, and she felt a sudden panic at the thought of it never having reached her. They came so rarely now, and such a long wait, this one the first in months, and short, she could feel, no more than a page, knowing already that she would be disappointed by it. Letters to one another becoming shorter and shorter over the years, a gulf widening between them and no way of bridging it properly, not when they lived such different lives, and always something to be said to Caroline, always some way of reprimanding her: "We can only pray that you have not come to regret the consequences of your decisions. You have always been headstrong, and would never listen to warning, though you were advised again and again against this marriage" and "You must know that I rarely speak of you now. Surely you must see that I cannot."

This letter beginning with news of the weather, written nine weeks since, so that they were in a different season now and the falling leaves that Cassandra detested were most likely under a layer of snow, the days shorter, colder, almost unimaginable in this heat. Still, she hunched over, pulled her arms in, as though she were cold, feeling that snowy air all around her. Cassandra excused the short letter, said

Caroline had more than likely guessed that she was with child again and as usual was somewhat unwell, but nothing very serious and it was already passing, the worst of it over. The doctor had been and given her some strengthening tonic so she was able most days to get about and do what was necessary. The baby was to be born, if she was correct, in February. She hoped for another girl, though the house had been rather too quiet since little Arthur had been sent to school and perhaps a boy would be nice, she was sure his papa would agree, though she didn't expect Caroline to understand. Feeling a sharp pain at that, then scanning the wishes for her health, folding the letter, putting it back in her purse, out of sight.

Looking up and down the avenue, taking in the convicts sweeping leaves nearby, cleaning the canal, the children running, nursemaids with toddlers and perambulators, an old man with two walking sticks, walking slowly, and a couple approaching, the woman with a Pomeranian on a leash, the dog giving small barks as it walked, yapping at everything it passed. They seemed not to notice, neither paying it any attention, unaware when it stopped to lift its leg, simply walking on, the dog urinating as it was dragged forward. She watched them pass, saw them go out the gate at the bottom of the avenue, past the guard house, St George's, could imagine their walk continuing in this way, down the Heerengracht, stopping at the Commercial Exchange, the library, shops along the way. And it was as though it were she and James walking, the two of them walking arm in arm, in silence, walking through the town, going to Reid's then, on one of those walks, that was when she had seen the bird; James who was with her, not Leah. James taking her on an excursion, getting her out of the house near the barracks, a little surprise for her, he'd said.

Opening the door for her, waiting for her to step inside before speaking of the creature he wanted to show her, a shrivelled thing of skin and bone, with wings, a furred body and wizened face, having heard of it from others and coming once or twice to look at it on his own, and now to show her, because it was impossible to believe unless one saw it. Leading her straight to it, pointing out the dusty bell jar at the back of the shop, the corner so dark that she had to squint to make out the features he had mentioned. He said he would have a lamp brought, called to Reid for light, more light, but she had already begun to wander off, walking through the oddities that filled every surface, hung from the ceiling, a crocodile, a rusty suit of armour, puffed out blow fish, jars of unborn infants, a baboon skull. Seeing the bird amongst them, its head a little back, chest pushed forward as though it were in song, its wings blue, outrageously blue, amongst the black. Asking if she might be permitted to touch it, just one of the blue feathers, only one, she'd be careful. But no, unfortunately, said Reid, it was a rare and very valuable item, he was afraid he could not allow it, not unless they were to purchase it first, of course. That had been in the early days, when they had no money to spare. Though she had not asked for it, did, in fact, not want it, only wished to look at it as it stood there, to feel the colour of it, James had become desperate, had felt he must buy her something, anything, picking up trays of insects, strange shrunken heads, weapons and skins, saying, "Look, here, isn't this interesting, shall I buy this for you, don't be shy, I will buy it, let me buy it for you." Shaking her head, smiling her discomfort, "No, nothing," but then Reid was joining in, "Perhaps the lady would like this or this," and James turned to her with that frantic look in his eyes, that imploring demand, "Well, do you want it? Is this what you want?"

Hearing laughter, looking up from her thoughts. Leah standing with three other slave apprentices, half-hidden behind an oak tree. It was she who was laughing, and the others, laughing in a little circle, grabbing hold of one another's arms and shoulders, shaking their heads as they did, Leah glancing across at the bench, seeming not to see Caroline watching them, drawing in her lips, speaking to her companions, her words ending in another burst of laughter.

Caroline hated her, hated the sound of her, the look on her face, the women around her. Wanted to call to her, humiliate her in front of them, demand that she come here at once, "You are to stand here with me, this is your place, here with me." Hating every part of her, those hands that were always on her, near her, ready to take hold of her. If only she had sold her when she had the chance, before this apprenticeship business began, before emancipation and all the rest, knowing she would have fetched a good price; girls with lighter complexions and straight hair were always in high demand. If only she had sold her, taken the money, boarded a ship, gone home.

She passed smallholdings, sharing the road with labourers going home at the end of the work day, but keeping her head down, pretending not to hear their greetings. Soon there were vineyards, neatly dotted with rosebushes at the end of each row. It was still early in the season, with grapes, small and green. Hunger moved her into the rows, made her take a bunch between thumb and forefinger of one hand, the other shading her eyes from the setting sun. The grapes dusty, hard at her touch, picking only one, rolling it clean against her dress before putting it in her mouth, her jaw aching at once with the sourness of it, the thick skin, the crunch of seeds, and she spat it out, sticking out her tongue, wiping it on her dress, then making her way back to the road, spitting again. Bunches on the road, taken by others and discarded, left to be crushed by hooves and wheels and feet. Birds and insects fed on that pulp, moving away lazily at the approach of people, returning after they had passed.

Coming to a village after a while, a gathering of cottages and gardens, smoke rising from chimneys as evening meals were being prepared. Moving away from the road again, this time finding a tree behind which she could sit, wanting to be out of sight. Watching as people came and went, a lady being driven in a carriage, an elderly man walking with a stick, children running with a ball.

A slave apprentice came close to where she sat, stood scratching his stomach. He looked at her, then took out a pipe and pouch of tobacco, beginning to fill the bowl of the pipe. Another approached, giving a loud greeting to the first. He said he was tired, had had enough, he was leaving, was going to leave in the night, he just had to gather his belongings, he'd not live another day if he didn't go, his master was trying to get everything out of him, every last drop that he could. "What does he care if he works me to death?" He interlinked his fingers, pushed his arms into the air, holding them there, moving his shoulders up and down. The first man lit his pipe, puffing on it as the other man finished stretching, then handed it to him, let him have his turn. "You don't know what will happen, they said we were free before and look what happened. What if they change their minds again and you get picked up as a runaway? What then? No, you'd better wait," he said. They looked across at where she sat, and she drew her feet in towards her, pulling her knees up, smoothing her skirt over them, her swollen ankle. The first man nodded at her. The second called to her, "And you, what do you think? Will this be it? Are we really going to be free this time?" She shook her head to show that she didn't know, then looked away. He tapped the bowl of the pipe clean, and they turned from her, walking back towards the village with slow steps.

There were empty bottles around her, some broken, and she held her hands around her knees, not wanting to cut herself on any shards that might be nearby. There were bones too, probably from the meals of farm labourers and slave apprentices who gathered here in the noontime shade. She was tempted to pick them up, to gnaw at whatever meat might be left on them, but she told herself to wait, that it had not yet come to that. Watching the sky darken into nightfall, the village soften with lamplight as people moved about their homes, spoke about their days, made plans for the next. The hours passed, lamps and fires going out, the village shrinking back into itself, leaving only the stars for her to move by.

She went quietly, walking with care along the cobbled streets, her feet, her ankle feeling strange with this change from the dirt track to smooth irregularity, feeling as though she might fall over, struggling to keep her balance. Yet managing to open the gates without there being any creaks, moving about the gardens as silently as she could. She had known before entering the village that she was going to steal, meaning to take only a little. But after the barren heat of the mountain and slopes, the gardens surprised her by being lush and full. Picking cucumbers, runner beans, tomatoes, gooseberries and blackberries, taking more than she could eat, thinking of nothing but her hunger, hunger that had been with her for years and years, all the years of her life. Never enough, always wishing for more, and now this bounty, this luxury, and she couldn't bring herself to stop.

A cottage stood at the outer reaches of the village, lamplight glowing inside, and she went up to the window, peering in. A freed man and woman sat at a table, working by the light of a single candle. The woman had a pile of clothes in a basket beside her, was mending them, bending forward over the table, holding the garments close to her face, smoothing them out, holding them up to the light, finding all the tears and gaps in need of repair. The man had nails between clenched lips, was hammering soles and uppers together, making shoes.

After a while he removed the nails from his mouth, stood

up and left the table, swinging his arms in circles, moving his head from side to side. A clock chimed on the mantle and he went towards it, opening the glass front and looking at the workings, blowing onto the clockface, moving one of the hands a little way with the tip of his forefinger.

The woman had looked up at his rising and finished the stitch she was on, then packed away her sewing and removed the basket to a corner of the room. The man came back to the table, put his tools away too. The woman went to a pot being kept warm with some coals in the fireplace and dished up for them, bringing the plates to the table. The man poured water for them from a beaker. They ate in silence, and when they had done, the woman stood up, reaching for his plate. Before she could take it, he had put his hand on hers, holding it there a moment and looking up into her face. The woman smiled, then turned away with the plates, the man picking up his tools again to return to work.

That gesture, the two of them working together long into the night, made something pull taut inside her, a string binding her to this place, this moment, to this cottage and this table. But more than that. It was stretching out to other places, to other moments and people, pulling painfully tight. It went all the way through every cottage in this village, every house she had passed, every home in which people lived, to that cottage of her own, the one she had been unable to imagine before when standing beside the blackfish, that cottage she had never had and could not believe she would ever have. It was September who had had the vision of it, though he had spoken of it only once and never again.

FIRST OF DECEMBER

It had been a cold day, raining. He had been sent out as usual to look for firewood on the mountain, coming back wet, smelling wild and fresh, the smell still on him late at night when at last she could get away from the inn and their master, finally coming to the barn to crawl in next to him in the straw where he was already asleep, his clothes hung up to dry on nails in the wall. Pushing against his skin, smelling the mountain on him, feeling his warmth. He rolled over to face her, kissing her, holding her against him, so dark that they couldn't see one another, only feel his lips right against hers, his breath on her face, talking of them having a cottage of their own, of working for no one but themselves, doing as they pleased.

He had promised nothing. It had not been a promise, she had known that, had always known that there was no promise. He had never said there would be a cottage, had never said he would come back for her. She had known he was married to a woman of his own faith, had known his wife, working alongside her until the master loaned her to his son when he got married and moved away. Every few months he allowed September to go and visit her and the child they had together. Watching him whittle toys for the boy, never speaking of him, but whittling those toys, growing restless in the days before he was allowed to leave. Coming back afterwards with a flower he had picked along the way, or a stone or seashell, something to show he had not forgotten her. But smelling different, and his arms loose around her during the nights that followed.

In those days, emancipation had felt like a threat, a thing

coming to separate them. But it had been worse than that, the way he had left, the way she had waited for him to come back, thinking he was coming, that they still had time. All these years and months waiting, for what? For what? And never a word, not until the washerwoman panted into the yard, coming to tell her that she had stopped to greet Shafik in the market, "he drives the wagon for Mr Goodes, you know, the one with the scar above his eyebrow, and you won't believe what he said, no you'll never guess, because he said he saw September, not at your master's son's farm with that wife of his, not in Cape Town or anywhere like that, no, all the way in Stellenbosch, that's where he was. Shafik saw him himself, with his own two eyes, saw him walking there along the main road as a free man, walking along and whistling, as though he had not a care in the world, not a single thing to worry about. And here you are, and there he is, and what do you have to say about that?"

Knowing then that she had to leave. Not to be with him, not to go and find him, nothing to do with him, only herself, herself, and this exact feeling now, of being pulled taut, and feeling everything in her, everything touching the world, and wanting to be part of it.

Friday
30th November 1838

Watching as labourers erected scaffolding, came and went with bricks and planks, hammering with nails clenched between their lips, passing up wood and tools to one another. Dust everywhere, a haze of it over the site as they sawed and planed, kicking up more of it when they walked, and it reached across the street to where he stood, tickled his throat, making him sneeze. Roused by that sneeze, by this busyness, this clouded air, and all of it his, all of it his doing.

Only the ground floor had been built so far, but already it was beginning to take on a certain presence, heralding the grandeur that was to come. Embellishments would be added later, had been ordered from back home, and he imagined them in place, the gable over the doorway, the flutes and spindles, scrolls and swags and statues, all of them white, with the façade painted a light blue. No detail would be missed by passersby, each decorative feature, the size and height of the building, all of it would be on display, ready for admiration, with no competition, neighboured only by a bland double storey in which an attorney, Mr Albany, lived, its façade embarrassingly out of date, still showing Dutch influences from the previous century. Chickens could be heard clucking in the backyard, and weeds grew from cracks in the front steps, some of them flowering, yellow and full-headed. A couple of pigeons moved amongst them, pecking at what could be found, while a ginger cat crouched nearby, leaning closer, ready to pounce. But then a hammer was dropped from the scaffolding, a man shouting, "Look out below!", others picking up his cry. The pigeons flew up at the noise, and the cat raised itself out of its crouch, stretched its hind legs, walked over to where they had been pecking, sniffed the ground, the weeds, then sat down and began to lick itself.

Ready to sneeze again at the dust raised by the fallen hammer and the flying pigeons, but holding it back, seeing Henry Borcherds and Major Cameron-Dow walking towards him from Wale Street. Lifting a hand in greeting, saying, "Well, gentlemen, what do you think?"

"A fine house," said Cameron-Dow. "Very fine indeed."

Borcherds agreed, saying he had just arrived from Simonstown for the party, that he was taking a stroll after the long carriage ride, had walked this way specifically to see what progress was being made with the building, and it certainly appeared to be coming along well since his last visit.

"Thank you, yes, I believe it is."

"More of this sort and we may well find ourselves with a half-decent town," said Cameron-Dow. "But there is so much that is dilapidated. Have you seen that monstrosity on Bree Street? The de Villiers set off for the interior and just left it to rot, and there's another, oh where is it, you know the one I mean, just around the corner here in Church Street, the one where..."

James was not listening, wanted to return the conversation to his new house, to himself, interrupting with, "Plenty of changes coming", meaning the bank, the tenements, his own plans and ideas, though Cameron-Dow misunderstood, said, "Indeed, indeed, never thought I would live to see the day, but here we are and bound to be a mess, bound to be a disaster, if only that vagrancy law had been passed, but they'll be lying about now, taking up the streets and nothing to be done about it, God save us. Philanthropy is a bugger of a thing, I tell you, Kendrick, an absolute bugger." He sighed, shook his head. "Well, good luck to you. We'll see you this evening", moving on up the street.

Borcherds shook hands with James, said, "Yes, see you this evening," then glanced around, speaking quietly. "I say, you haven't wanted to reconsider, perhaps postpone to another day when things are less…?"

James laughed. "Oh, no need for that, no need, I assure you. I have the governor's word, and Major Cameron-Dow's too, they have both assured me there will be a full military presence. We will be quite safe."

Borcherds nodded. "Anyhow, I'd say it all looks peaceful enough so far, doesn't it?"

"Perfectly so," said James. "Nothing out of the ordinary."

But the men were sluggish, he could see that, working with reluctance, ignoring the foreman, rolling their eyes at his instructions, joking loudly amongst themselves. Progress was slow and he crossed the street, ready to speak to them, to tell them they need not return the next day, that there would be any number of men coming in from the farms and countryside looking for work, willing to do it for less pay. Going through the bare entranceway, his feet crunching on the floor, dust covering his shoes, lifting up towards him, and once more the tickle in his nose, putting up his handkerchief, blowing out something ochre-coloured, thick as blood.

The foreman saw him enter, took the opportunity to begin shouting at a man who was bending slowly, picking up a few nails he had spilled, taking them one at a time, placing them in his pocket. The man did not respond to the shouts, kept bending and rising, bending and rising without expression. Then came the booming shot of the noon day gun on Signal Hill, always a surprise, making James start, look around for danger. Some of the men had similar reactions, but most of them, the Mohammedans, climbed down from the scaffolding, put down their tools, orientated themselves, fell to the ground as they began their heathen prayers. They were facing him, were prostrate before him, as though it were to him they were praying, he the object of their worship. Irritation gave way to something like affection for these filthy, lazy men, feeling his hand rise towards them in benediction. After all, were they not his to bless? Was he not building houses for them? Giving them jobs, giving them a bank, building a city around them?

The rain came hard and sudden, and no roof, no ceiling, nothing to act as cover, the men caught off guard, clasping hold of the scaffolding to keep from falling. Wood slick, their clothes drenched, everything soaking wet almost at once. Some of the Mohammedans staying down long enough to finish their prayers, but many jumped up, looking for cover. In the centre of the room a large pool was spreading out across the floor, the rain sending up fierce splashes where it fell. James tried at first to stand in one of the doorways, alongside the foreman, a few of the workers, but it gave no shelter and the smell of them was foul. He ran out into the street away from them, stomping wide-legged through the mud, holding his hat down as rain fell in his eyes, the stink of old urine lifting with the downpour. Others were running for shelter too and he had to go carefully to keep from colliding with them, swerving when a slave apprentice came to a sudden halt in front of him, turning her scarfed head up to the sky, calling, "See His tears, see how He cries for what has been done to us!"

Dogs bayed behind her. She was not fast enough, slipping on the muddy ground as she tried to get away, and they were upon her, one on her back, others at her thighs, jumping up, knocking her over, pushing wet snouts into her face, into her open mouth, sniffing her, their tails wagging. She stopped the scream that had been coming, lay back, began to laugh at the tickling, warm tongues, even held her hands out for them to lick the rain from her.

"Lurcher, Keeper, all of you, stop it! Come here, come back, stop that!" A young slave apprentice in a conical hat came jogging up the hill. He had fallen too, his knees stained with mud and grass, his arms muddied to the elbows. The dogs turned to look at him, a couple of them running to him as he approached, wagging their tails, running back to her. She was sitting now, trying to tame the mess of her hair, straighten her dress where it had come up over her knees. He called to her, "Are you hurt? Did they hurt you?"

She shook her head and he stopped running, leaned forward, hands on thighs, catching his breath, walking the last steps to her, then pulling the dogs by their collars, saying, "Get off, you pests, get off." They moved away from her, continuing to wag their tails, scattering into the long grass, their coats smeared with dark stripes of wet, catching raindrops and petalled weeds on their hanging ears.

He looked up at the grey sky, his hat keeping the view from him so that he had to tip further backwards than was natural, rain falling into his face, and he grimaced, wiping at his eyes with a muddied hand, turning back to where she lay, holding the same hand out to her, helping her up and across to a large oak tree, the leaves young and brilliant, painfully bright against the sullen sky, drops running down the trunk of the tree, dripping from the leaves and branches. She stood silently, wiping the mud that had been transferred from his hand to hers on the back of her dress so that he wouldn't see. But he was watching her, noticed her torn clothes, her bound ankle, the stains on her dress, the scabs across her arms and face.

Again, "Did they hurt you?"

Again she shook her head.

"Are you sure? You have no pain, no injury?"

"Really, it wasn't them. I fell a few days ago, that's all. You don't need to worry."

Throwing himself down on the ground with a sigh, lying back, his chest heaving, still catching his breath. "I thought I'd lost them, they just shot off after you. They're young and they get too excited and then they don't listen. When you ran like that they thought you were playing with them, a game, you know. You shouldn't have run. Remember that for next time. Dogs will always chase you if you run." Pausing, then, "Were you very scared?"

"At first."

"Sorry."

He had his breath back, sat up, leaning against the trunk, wiping mud from his trousers, his arms. She could hear the grit of the mud moving against his skin, feeling it on her own where he had touched her, watching as he stood and went to the edge of the tree's canopy, holding out his arms into the rain, letting the drops fall onto him until he thought he had enough, wiping at the mud again, spreading the dirt, and he shook his head, coming back under the branches, wiping his hands as best he could on his shirt and trousers.

She pointed in the direction of the dogs, "All of them, they're all yours?"

"No, no, I just look after them. They're bred for hunting down that way near the military base at Wynberg and I feed them and exercise them, and I help to train them." He laughed. "But that takes time and I'm still learning." Putting both thumbs into the waistband of his trousers, hitching them up, breathing out heavily. "I really thought I'd lost them when they went off like that, and Jesus, I was thinking, please save me Jesus, because if I lost them there would have been a whipping like no other."

"I'm sorry."

"Well, they're here now."

Putting his hand round his back, feeling for something in his shirt, bringing out a hunk of bread, breaking it in two and standing for a moment looking at the two halves. She lowered herself down onto a root, her skirt thin and wet, feeling the damp against her, the rough of the bark. The dogs had come running at the smell of food and he held one half aloft, stretching over their heads to pass it to her. She pushed herself up, reaching for it, feeling the warmth of it from being kept against his skin, the crust damp from the rain on his shirt, eating with her hands over her mouth to stop the dogs from getting to it.

"Just give them a shove when they're annoying you," he said, pushing one of them away where it was sniffing at her hands. But she didn't want that, purposely allowed crumbs to fall so that they would come back, lick them up, stay with her. Rubbing their heads, their backs, their fur coming off on her palms, all the different shades of them. Scratching behind their ears, feeling their hot breaths, smelling the animal wetness of them.

"That's Sprinter," he said, his mouth full, and she leaned forward to hear better. "Here's Spoiler, and Trooper over there. And this one is Loper. He has dreams when he sleeps and he kicks and whimpers like this," mimicking the movements and sounds, lying on his side, twitching his arms and legs, the dog taking advantage of his closed eyes to steal the bread from his hand and run off with it, the others chasing after him, barking and howling. He shrugged and laughed. "Ah, there it is, there you have it, I never seem to learn."

She still had some of her bread left and held it out to him. He waved a hand, shook his head. "No, no, you eat it. It's for you, there's more for me when I get back, my mother works in the kitchens."

He waited until she had finished eating, then said he had to get the dogs back, he had stayed out longer than he should have, and it was no good avoiding one whipping only to get another. He asked which way she was going, and she pointed left, down towards the wagon road.

"Cape Town?"

She nodded.

"We'll go part of the way with you, just until we get to the path back to Wynberg." Whistling for the dogs, calling their names, saying "behave yourselves" as they ran up, though they were obedient now. "Are we all here? Are we ready?"

Looking at the dogs, counting them off, then looking at her, "Do you have everything?" Seeing her pick up her small pack, her cloak wet through, water running from her hair onto her forehead. Taking off his hat, untying it from under his chin, saying, "One moment, just a second, let me get this," holding it out to her, indicating the sky with his chin, "For the rain. It helps with the sun too." She was surprised by his hair, the streaks of grey in it despite his youth, and she felt that she couldn't accept the hat, that it belonged to him, to cover up up the grey, the age which was being made rapid in him. But he placed it on her head, flicked the strings from behind her ears, said, "Its better if you tie it yourself."

There was smell of sweat in the hat, a smell of dog and rain. She brought the strings together under her chin, drew them tight against her, feeling the pressure of them on her skin, tilting her head to keep the scent of him near her as they walked, dogs on either side, nudging her hands from time to time, giving a jump of excitement, running off, running back. All the while listening to him talk, about the dogs, what they ate, what this one did and that one, details of their pedigree, their parents, and what you could tell from the shape of the head, the way the tail hung, then, nearing the wagon road, stopping, saying, "Do you know what I'm going to do?"

Shaking her head, feeling the strange sensation of the hat moving with her.

"Tomorrow, as soon as we get to midnight, the minute that church clock starts striking midnight, do you know what I'm going to do?"

"No."

"Change my name. I'm going to change it right then

and there, and then everyone will know I'm free. Every time people say my name, every time they hear it or think of me, they will know I'm a free man."

"What will you change it to?"

"I'm still deciding. Geseënd or Verhoogd, one of those. What do you think? Which is more like the name of a free man?

"I don't know. Maybe Verhoogd."

"Yes, that's what I was thinking too, that's who I am going to be. Verhoogd the free man. That's me from tomorrow at midnight."

She wondered what she might change her name to and whether it would matter when she had no one to tell it to, remembering the dead man on the mountain, the scrap of paper she had left beside him, the way it had flapped in the wind.

FIRST OF DECEMBER

All morning she had lain in bed, had been told to rest, that she must not exert herself before the party. Paging through the Ladies Pocket Magazine, calling Leah to bring tea, to adjust the curtains, open the window. People and carts moving about the town streets as usual, a steady whirl of greetings and conversations, and for a while the same lone voice passing back and forth beneath her window, repeating the chorus of a Dutch hymn. Then from somewhere further along there came shouting, and "freedom" she heard from one of the voices, "never again set foot" from another, recognising it to be Mr Sellars from three doors down. Getting up, going to the open window, peering out into a strangely overcast day, everything grey and heavy, but no time to wonder at it, because there was more shouting, carriage drivers now, and men with handcarts and barrows, "get out of the way, you fool, move, go on," as a slave apprentice stood in the dust of the street, pulling off his jacket, throwing it to the ground, kicking it as he removed his shirt, tore it to pieces, flinging the bits towards Sellars's house, though they did not go far, fell limp into the street a few feet away. Standing there bare-chested, picking up the pieces, throwing them again, shouting all the while, but she could make out none of it, did not know what his grievance was. Soldiers were moving in through the crowded street, two of them grabbing hold of his arms, the others hurrying people along, but everyone was watching, had stopped to see what would happen, the man continuing to shout, and someone she could not see called out to him from the street or a window, again in a language she could not understand.

Watching him being led away, a small crowd following, and "should have waited for tomorrow" she heard someone say as they rounded the corner.

Returning to bed, to her magazine, the hymn being taken up again outside, fading in and out as the carriages came and went, as hawkers called, and then the trundle of the dogcart, the baker's boy adding to the calls that he had rolls, fresh rolls. Picturing him before her, his cap, his tattered trousers and bare feet, his scabby mouth singling out individuals, "Lady with the fan, hey lady, you want? Mister, oi, mister, don't be shy, they're fresh, just baked, fresh and ready to eat." Seeing him often on her walks up the Avenue, only once having the courage to whisper to Leah to buy a roll for her. It had been autumn, the Avenue filled with dry leaves, a couple of convicts sweeping them into piles, sweeping and sweeping, the leaves continuing to fall around them. Eating the bread where she stood, eating it with her hands, glancing around for someone to tell, someone to whom she could say, "Look at me, I am eating this bread and it is delicious." Ringing now for Leah that she might be sent to run after him, bring back a roll, maybe even two, ringing so hard in her eagerness that she did not notice the rain start, only when Leah pointed it out as she entered, saying, "Whoever heard of this, rain in November?" Closing the window in haste, then rushing through the rest of the house doing the same in other rooms.

Lying there for hours, listening to the rain, as hard as a winter storm, hail against the windows, the glass ready to crack, hours of it as she lay dozing, hearing it in her sleep, and she was wading through water, swept up by it, carried out, far out into the deep sea, was being taken under, overpowered by it, with no one to hear her call.

Then James was saying her name, rousing her from the flood. He was wet, his hands wet on her, and she struggled awake, felt the water still in her lungs, was coughing, coughing, did not know at once that she was in her bedroom, thought herself upon that filthy shore, thought herself dead and drowned.

"Here, look, I have a gift for you, I had it especially made for you," he said, holding out a large package, the paper marked with raindrops. "Come, sit up, open it, open it."

The room dark from the overcast sky, and still coughing, straining for breath, unable to see properly, fumbling with the string, letting it fall a few times, and he grew frustrated, taking it from her, ripping the paper, pulling the string to the side and then off. "Look," he said, shaking it out, holding it up for her to see. A dress. White silk, with flowers of pale pink at the bodice and skirt. A replica of the one he had spoken of before, made for their engagement party, and long since out of fashion. "See, do you see? I spared no expense, less than a day it took, and I spared no expense."

She felt the waves around her, the water in her lungs, the dress hanging before her like an anchor.

Brushing his hat where dust had covered it, had made a paste with the rain, bristle marks showing starkly on the crown and brim. Knowing he should wait until it had dried, that he was only making it worse, but continuing nonetheless, enjoying the briskness of the motion.

Moving across to the window as he brushed, looking out into the rain-wet street, the noise, the vendors, the bodies rushing about. Sunset coming, shadows long, and already a low star in a patch of unclouded sky, winking pallidly as it rose into the waiting night.

FIRST OF DECEMBER

Leah helped her on with her undergarments, dressed her hair, the curling tongs hot against her cheek and neck, smell of burning sharp in her nose, tasting it even, feeling that bitterness across her tongue and at the back of her throat, telling Leah to stop, to wait a few moments, to fan her head and chest. Leah doing so for a little while, then glancing at the clock on the mantle, "Oh, that isn't the time!", handing the fan to Caroline, saying they could do the last of the curls afterwards, just a minute, she would be back in a minute, and "Look how beautiful," bringing the dress from the small room beside the kitchen where she had gone over it earlier with a clothes iron. Laying it on the bed now, carrying a stool to where Caroline stood in front of the mirror, then going back for the dress, lifting it carefully, saying "Here we go, are you ready, arms up, here it comes," pulling it wide so that it would not disrupt her hair. Feeling the weight of it at once, the mass of material and ribbons, of bows and flowered garlands, all of them coming down over her, too much, far too much, and hanging loosely once on, the seamstress having worked to measurements from before her illness: bodice drooping, sleeves slipping down, the weight of the dress resting in her elbows, cutting into her, pulling her to the ground.

"Don't fret, miss, we'll make it work," said Leah, going from the room again, leaving Caroline to hold this burden, this engulfing onerous past, feeling herself back at her engagement, at the joy she had felt, the light inside her, with James, her James, beside her, love for him alive and beating throughout her, and what was it now, this regret and yearning, this painful thing, was it love, could she still call it that?

Leah back with a sewing basket, digging through it for the right colour thread, for a sharp needle, putting the end of the thread in her mouth, wetting it, bringing it to a point so that she could pass it through the eye of the needle. Having to try a few times, the room too dark, moving across to the lamp, trying again and succeeding. "This will do the trick, miss, just you wait and see," pinching the fabric together, creating gathers and pleats where they would not look odd, fixing them in place with pins, before coming back with the needle, making quick small stitches, sewing her into the dress. Caroline feeling the fabric tighten around her, water in her lungs again, being dragged down, far down, squeezed on all sides, beginning to drown.

Midnight
First of December
1838

The rain had continued all day, had not relented, and at the last minute he had to borrow umbrellas where he could, purchasing others at prices he would not usually have considered, then had to hire a dozen male apprentices to hold them, wait for the carriages to arrive, escort the guests up the stairs of the Exchange, keeping them dry as best they could. There had to be girls too, given rags, down on their knees wiping down the stone floor after each guest had come through. Even so, Mrs Fraser had slipped, her husband catching her just too late. A chair was brought to her, everyone gathering around, but she had not been injured, was able to laugh, revived by a small glass of sweet wine. That had been the only disaster, soon forgotten.

Inside, the banquet room had none of the recycled decorations used season after season for subscriptions balls, always smelling of dust and mould. Everyone commented on the change, how they would not have known this to be the same place, wasn't it splendid, just wonderful, quite enchanting what Mr Kendrick had done. The military band played at one end of the room, with an area kept open beside them for dancing, and at the other end a long table, made longer than usual by the addition of several smaller tables, all of them overlaid with the same extraordinary tablecloth that seemed to go on for miles, comprising yards and yards of imported fabric. Places were set with matching glasses, silverware, plates and chargers, and if the chairs were not identical, no one could tell, each draped in the same green velvet cover. Sideboards had been made for the occasion, already bearing a plaque stating James's name, the date, his generosity in donating them to the Exchange. Upon them were cups and saucers, multiple silver tea sets, polished candelabra, bunches of hothouse flowers, picked fresh that morning. More velvet hung in swags over the doors and windows, while a brand-new crystal chandelier sparkled in the ceiling. Each of the nine courses was brought out by a team of waiters, another team seeing to the wines and brandies. In all, there was a surplus of the best the Cape had to offer, as well as much that had been imported.

The guests dined amidst laughter, twisting, turning to see who was seated where and beside whom, waving, oh there you are, isn't this a treat, have you tried the veal, have you seen the chandelier, such extravagance, such an unforgettable pleasure! Greeting him with applause as he rose to give his speech, calling out his name, words of praise. He smiled indulgently, raising a hand to ask for silence. "You know me to be a man of action," he said. "Action is the key, nothing changes without motion, always there must be movement, a movement forward. That is what we are witnessing now, indeed we have been witnessing it these past several years. There's a great change sweeping the world, but more especially this colony, already we have seen how emancipation has brought wealth, and it will bring more, that is undeniable. Bigger, better opportunities are waiting for all of us, such as my new venture, the First Colonial Bank, founded under my name but looking for further investors, and I sincerely hope that you will join me in this forward movement, that you will take up your places beside me in this new future that is waiting for us all."

Judge Campbell allowed the cheers to die down, then

clanged his knife against his glass, said he had a few words to add, if they didn't mind, he would make sure to be brief. It was an honour, he said, for the Cape to have so fine a man, that he was certain he spoke for everyone whether present or absent, and that when times were unsettled as they were, there was great comfort in men like him. The bank was an excellent idea, he certainly would be adding his name to the list of investors, and urged others to do the same. Already the guests were rising, draining their glasses, drinking the health of Kendrick, of the Cape, of the First Colonial Bank.

But as midnight approached, they began to quieten. The dishes were empty, eight of the courses complete. They whispered amongst themselves, or sat in silence, uncertain of what was to be expected upon the hour. Someone had gone outside for a breath of fresh air, to check on the rain, and that someone, though no one could quite say who it was, they had only heard, it was being passed around, that he had seen horrible things going on in the streets, buildings being burnt to the ground, hordes of slaves armed with knives slaughtering anyone they came upon. The ladies were alarmed, some of them began to cry, their husbands muttering to one another that it had been damned foolish to have a party on this night of all nights, damned foolish. But the governor spoke with Major Cameron-Dow who could confirm that there was a strong military presence on the streets, that there had been no reports of violence, only a bit of noise, a bit of jollity, but nothing worse than any other Friday night. There would be an armed escort for every guest when they left. There was nothing to fear. Still, they seemed hesitant, wondering whether to leave at once, or bar the doors to the Exchange, hide inside. James went around reassuring everyone, genial and calm, bringing them back to the table for dessert. It was not long before they had returned to eating, exclaiming at the array of sweets on offer, and soon they had forgotten their fears, were a little drunk, the flowers drooping, petals falling onto the tablecloth in clusters. Brows were sweaty, the room warm. They neglected their manners, had elbows on the tables, or picked idly at dishes with their fingers, licking off the cream.

Caroline waited for the last dish to be cleared before she asked whether she might be excused. He had watched her move amongst the guests for hours, seen how she smiled, how she charmed them. This was not the stammering, shy woman she had been of late. It was the dress that had caused this change, he knew, the dress that had been a sensation, drawing compliments from every corner, and he had taken her around, shown her off, listened to her say more than once, "Oh yes, it was quite a surprise, he does spoil me so." This was her as he had known her, the healthy, laughing girl with whom he had once made quick, laughing love in the inn beside a railway station, who had kissed his scarred forehead in Hyde Park.

He walked out with her, holding an umbrella as she got into the carriage, helping to fold the profusion of gown around her legs, then passed the umbrella to the guard who was to accompany her, before calling for another to come and sit beside the driver. "We can't be too safe," he said. Really he wished to be going with her, wished to draw her to him, kiss her. But there was another memory, stronger than the others, of him embracing her, neither with force or violence, only with love, he had not even kissed her, only had her in his arms, and she had pushed him away, crying, "I don't want this, I don't want it, please."

The rain came down hard again, and despite the umbrella, she was getting wet, had raindrops driving into her face. He felt in his pocket for a handkerchief, finding instead the brass button he had been carrying with him all week. Each day he had moved it from one jacket to another, able to give himself no reason for this action, but doing it nonetheless. On an impulse he wanted to give it to her, remembering, it seemed years ago, how they had watched the branded man finding it in the shallows, and then, later, on his own, seeing the woman drop it, search for it, how he had picked it up afterwards, saw, for a moment, Caroline gazing with what he had thought to be love. But then the carriage was moving, and he was being called back inside, the governor wishing to speak to him. He felt once more that irresistible urgency moving within him, driving him back up the stairs into the light and noise.

The carriage moved slower than expected, the streets full, people standing in groups, holding hands, walking in processions, some of them singing, "Victoria! Victoria!", waving handkerchiefs, a few with faded Union Jacks, pulling up skirts or trousers to dance a jig, making a point of showing their shod feet. Children peered from windows, their mothers coming to pull them away, while near the church a man blew a battered trumpet, another played a stringed instrument made from a gourd. Beside them a woman had taken the washing basket from her head, emptied the contents onto the street, climbed into it, saying, "Now we rest, now is the time for resting."

The guard did not turn to look at Caroline, kept his eyes to the right, the other, in the driver's seat, looking to the left. The first still held the umbrella, the horses' trot jolting his arm so that he held it unsteadily, rain dripping down her neck, along her back, and more of it coming from the front, driving into her face, soaking her lap. She clutched the material at her knees, trying to wring it out a little, and the guard, misunderstanding the gesture, saying, "No need to be afraid, Mrs Kendrick, they won't dare try anything with us here, you'll be quite safe with us."

But she felt no fear, saw no danger, wanted, in fact, to get out of the carriage and join the celebrations, to move about as she had once before, a time long forgotten, at Cassandra's wedding, feeling stirred by something bold and wonderful, having it move within her, spill out of her, wide and wide and wide. Several men wishing to dance with her, and having to feign interest to calm her parents' fears about James, all the while a letter in her corset from him in Bristol, writing that he was trying to raise funds, that he had an opportunity, a certain prospect, the letter already worn thin with handling, knowing that she would marry him, had as good as said she would, no matter her family's opposition.

Sometimes now still that feeling, that stirring joy, even tonight, watching him in moments of silence, his face clear, without anger. And here, this noise, this excitement, these streets, who else did she wish to share them with, who else to tell of church bells beginning to chime the hour, peeling from St George's, the Dutch church, all the other churches around the town, with voices singing out loudly from the mosque on the hill? All these rhythms, out of time with one another, crowds counting in the streets, and she could not follow along, arriving at her doorstep having counted somewhere between eight and fifteen.

The guard lifting her down, the other stretching to hold the umbrella, and "Quickly now, quickly, let us get you out of this rain", but she asked if they might wait a moment, standing on the doorstep to hear the last of the chimes, the Mohammedan's call rising up, bells swinging, swinging, never stopping. Then staring up in surprise, giving a little start, even the guard stepping forward thinking it a threat, an attack, as fireworks burst across the sky near the mountain. Needing to tell someone, to have someone see it, knocking on the front door for Leah, "Come, hurry, come see the fireworks!"

There was no reply and she looked for the key in her purse, not finding it at first, then bringing it out, her gloves wet, fingers slipping on the metal as she tried to push it into the lock, but missing, once, twice, the guard taking it from her, water dripping from the brim of his hat, and he stepped aside for her to enter, waiting as she called into the hallway, "Leah, the lamp, where's the lamp?" Stopping to apologise to him for the darkness, for having to wait, then calling again, "Leah, where are you? I'm back, I'm here, where's the lamp?" He found one on the entrance table, lit it, saying he had to go, there would be others needing to be escorted home, would she be all right if he left her now? Yes, Leah was here somewhere, she'd be all right, thanking him, telling him to be safe, to get dry, then locking the door behind him, the key moving more easily after she had removed her gloves. Taking the lamp down the passage to the kitchen, "Leah, what are you doing? You've missed it all. Are you here? I'm wet through, this rain... Are you—" Seeing the back door standing open, putting her head out into the backyard where the slave quarters were, no sign of light coming from them, thinking Leah had fallen asleep, wondering how it was possible to sleep on such a night. Calling for her one last time, then going inside, beginning to feel the chill of wetness, wishing for tea, but finding the fireplace cold, and not knowing how to do it herself.

Going up to her room, sitting on the edge of the bed, the dress uncomfortable around her, all night the weight of it, the dreadful, overwhelming weight, made worse now with rain. Leaning back with a sigh, her hand sliding a little along the quilt, fingertips brushing against something, picking it up, holding it to the flame: the purse in which Leah's money was kept. Knowing without opening it that it was empty, knowing too that Leah was not asleep, had not slipped out to join in the celebrations, that she had gone and that she would not return.

Starting to shiver, throwing down the purse, going across the room with the lamp, needing to get this dress off, needing to take it off, the dreadful, suffocating weight of it. Looking into the mirror for any sign of the thread Leah had used to sew her into it, anything to pull or tear, but finding nothing, just a froth of white, of flounces pulling her down into the deep, far into the flood from which there was no escape.

FIRST OF DECEMBER

She had not arrived in Cape Town alone. For much of the day had taken shelter from the rain, loitering beneath trees that lined the wagon road, once leaning against an abandoned hut, the door stuck fast, hinges old and rusted. Tired by then, already wet through, sodden clothes chafing under her arms, at her neck, skin rubbed raw, having to take off the hat so that she could rest her head against the door. Placing it over her face, tying it at the back of her head, her fingers wrinkled and white, struggling to make a knot. Light coming murkily through the weaving, closing her eyes to it, taking deep breaths of the thick wet cone of air. For a time dozing fitfully, the dogs back, licking her hands, jumping up on her, reaching out to stroke them, finding nothing, then lifting the hat from her face, the smell of them still strong on her.

Lured into the rain again in the early evening by the sound of singing, her feet slipping in the mud, growing thick where it clung to her in chunks. Reaching the road in time to see a wagon already in the distance, hearing the fading song that had come from its passengers, listening for the words that she could not make out, and stepping blindly into a deep rut where one of the wheels had passed, twisting her bound ankle. Standing still a moment, waiting for the pain, but it did not come, and she pulled her foot out, yellow with the clutching mud.

Others moved slowly through the downpour, their backs laden with belongings, some of them were singing, having picked up the song that had passed them, most of them softly, but one, an old woman, singing loudly as she walked, interrupting herself to call greetings to everyone she saw. Behind her a man with scars on his face, three fingers missing from his right hand, and a pregnant woman with two small children who were skipping along, singing, "We're free, we're free!" Even as they passed soldiers standing with rifles and glaring at them, the children sang, their mother trying to hush them, saying, "Not now, not yet." There were others with rifles too, men standing guard in front of their houses, or patrolling their grounds. The old woman called to one of them, "What do you need that for? What do you think I'm going to do to you? Are you afraid of me? You think I'm going to hurt you? Is that what you think?"

The man ignored her, looked up and down the road, shifting his rifle a little when he saw another wagon approach. It was full, as the first had been, the passengers singing, most of them standing, holding onto one another or to the side, raising an arm from time to time to wave to passersby, inviting them to climb up and join them. They stopped when they saw the group walking in the rain, saying, "Get in, get in, we're all going the same way," helping first the children and their pregnant mother, then the old woman, and the man. Coming to her last, reaching out to where she had stepped aside. "Come on, there's plenty of room, don't be shy." Pulling her up onto the dirty wagon bed, and she sat at the edge, on top of muddy footprints, leaving her own feet dangling, watching the road dissolve into wetness behind her, the rifled men growing smaller and smaller as the jolting rhythm of the wagon knocked the mud from her feet.

The town came to them out of the dark, everything around them long since in shadow, the people they passed invisible, knowing of their presence only by the voices that rose up to echo their own hoarse chorus. As the town appeared, someone shouted, "Praise be to Jesus, we are here," others joining in, "Praise Him, praise Jesus, praise the Father, we've arrived." She felt it too, the need to honour someone, to shout it into the shimmering light of the rain-drenched town. "Praise, praise," she said. She had lost the hat somewhere along the way, was soaked through, but didn't mind, was caught in the glow of buildings all around, windows lamplit, thronging with people, and then she was being pulled to her feet as the wagon jolted further into the heart of the town. She had never seen anything like it, felt breathless at the height of the buildings, the unending expanse of lanes and streets going off into further streams of dull light, everything flushed and pulsing warm. People filled the streets, some of them dancing beside the trundling wagons which seemed at a standstill. The town heaving with the movement of all these bodies, taking a deep breath in, and she felt it exhale into her, felt her pulse rise, her breast fill, all of her scars, all of her wounds filling with that vibrant light, and she was rising upwards, being raised high, even as she was being lifted from the carriage and brought to the ground, even then she was rising, thrust among a thousand other breaths and pulses, all of them wet and dazzling.

New this feeling, new this place, standing now in St George's, not knowing how she had come to be there, but full, so full, lifting her voice to their prayers, holding her arms up towards the high ceilings, watching the sway of candlelight on the walls, feeling the cool smooth stone beneath her aching dirty feet. Tight against her neighbours' backs, their wet hair, their damp clothes, and they were holding her hand, smiling at her, touching her shoulders, her face, clasping her to them, calling her sister, kissing her cheeks. "Jesus," they said, "Oh God our Father", speaking to Him and to their ancestors, to anyone who would listen, anyone they could think of, mothers and fathers and siblings and children, all those who had not made it to this moment.

Then, all at once, a great hush, everyone quiet as the church bell began to strike the hour, people falling to their knees, raising their hands, counting the strikes, grabbing hold of one another. Falling to her knees beside them, beginning to cry. All the loneliness of those days in the wilderness, and of all the years before that, of her dead baby, of September gone, all the loneliness rushing out of her, thrust into this stirring communion, waiting for that final strike, the stroke of midnight, and there it was, a great cheer rising up, this joyful agony that at last it was here, this thing that had been promised and promised and seemed would never come. Cries of hallelujah, hallelujah filling the church, a cry of life, a cry to live. She wanted to start at once, did not want to wait any longer, wanted to take this pulsing, glowing light outside and live, pushing her way past them, these faces, these clutching hands, bright with joy, and knowing only that she had to go, she had to get outside and start. Coming out into the rain, the fresh night, everything washed clean, walking down the stone steps of the church, out into her freedom, and having nowhere to go.

With thanks to Johan Fourie and my wonderful former colleagues at LEAP, Stellenbosch University. Thank you, too, to Robert Peett for holding my hand through the horrors of writing.